IMPOSSIBLE MATCH

Becky Barker

A KISMET® Romance

METEOR PUBLISHING CORPORATION
Bensalem, Pennsylvania

To Amanda, lovable Amanda. I expect the favor to be returned someday. Love Mom.

BECKY BARKER

Becky Barker lives in Ohio with her husband, Buzz, and their three teenagers: Rachel, Amanda, and Thad. She's an avid reader of romances and considers herself one of those lucky people whose life has been filled with music, laughter, and love. She enjoys hearing from readers and can be reached by writing: P. O. Box 113, Mt. Sterling, Ohio 43143.

Other books by Becky Barker:

PROLOGUE

Tyler Brogan shook hands with Aaron Cameron across the older man's desk.

"Have a seat, Mr. Brogan," Aaron suggested while making a quick appraisal of his guest. Here was a man who made things happen. There was no sign of softness in the dark eyes and firm jaw line. His handshake and proud bearing proclaimed a self-confidence that Aaron was willing to bet had been gained through experience and hard knocks.

For an instant he thought the younger man might refuse the invitation to sit, but then they both settled into chairs and continued an intense perusal of each other.

Aaron's innate ability to judge a man's character was one of the reasons for his phenomenal success in the business world. His wealth and power were legendary. It wouldn't be unusual for an ambitious executive to seek him out, yet the man facing him claimed to have come on personal business. Aaron still hadn't a clue as to why the young California executive should seek him out, but his curiosity was thoroughly aroused.

"When I spoke with you on the phone you said you had a private matter to discuss with me," Aaron began. "I'll confess, I'm intrigued. Should I know you?"

Ty gave a terse shake of his head. "You don't know me, and until a month ago I knew of you only through your business reputation." Tension was evident in the rugged features of his face and rigid set of his shoulders as he began to explain.

"My mother asked me to get in touch with you. In fact, I made her a deathbed promise. She was battling a fatal illness and was in a great deal of pain. She sometimes hallucinated, but she was adamant that I find you and have you corroborate her story."

Aaron nodded. He was a man who kept promises and respected the code of honor in others. His curiosity intensified. "What was your mother's name?"

"Sarah Brogan, but if what she told me is true, you would have known her by her maiden name, Sarah Halloway."

Ty watched intently as Aaron's eyes widened and grew dark with emotion. Tyler was an expert at seeing through phoney reactions, but Cameron's reaction was genuine. His blood chilled.

Aaron could never forget Sarah Halloway. Despite the fact that he hadn't seen his old girlfriend for nearly thirty-three years, she'd been his first love, and he'd been her first lover.

"I remember your mother well," Aaron replied. "We were engaged to be married when I joined the army, but she jilted me for another man. At the time I thought I would die of a broken heart or find some way to win her back, but I did neither."

Ty's naturally dark skin grew pale. It wasn't the answer he'd hoped to hear. Intense emotional strain was clearly visible on his strong features. He gripped the arms of his chair with huge hands, his knuckles white.

"She told me that you were my natural father," he proclaimed bluntly, his displeasure evident in his ragged tone. "My dad has been dead for a year. When faced with my mother's death and her insistence that my biological father was still living, I promised to see you just to pacify her. I only wanted to honor her wish." His tone hardened. "I really hadn't expected you to admit you'd known her."

Aaron had gone pale, too. He looked closer into eyes just a shade darker than his own brown. Brogan's thick, dark hair lacked streaks of gray but was the color and texture of his own. Brogan was taller and more solidly built, but there wasn't that much difference in their size and frame.

"When were you born?" Aaron asked, his voice rough.

Ty closed his eyes and dragged in a deep breath. If Aaron Cameron wanted to know his date of birth, then there was a strong possibility his mother had told him the truth. He gave the older man the month and year and then stared directly into his eyes as he watched the mental calculation.

Aaron was shaken but tried to retain control of his

emotions. "I was with your mother nine months before your birth," he declared. "I did officer's training in California and lived there for several months. Then I was sent to Vietnam. She wanted to get married, but I asked her to wait. I was stunned when I got her Dear John letter and learned she was marrying someone else."

Ty looked down at his hands, loosened his grip on the chair, and was annoyed at the tremor that shook him. His mother had been a proud woman. She'd loved Aaron Cameron, but had refused to trap him with the knowledge of her pregnancy.

That's the way she'd explained it, and Aaron seemed to be confirming her story, but Ty still didn't want to believe it. He'd loved and respected his dad, despite their differences. He still grieved—for his dad, his mother, and the absolute trust he'd given them. Why had they never trusted him with the truth?

"Did she tell you that she married your father because she was pregnant with my child?" Aaron forced himself to ask.

Their eyes locked and tension between them was almost palpable. Neither could deny the facts, yet neither was prepared to accept such a devastating truth.

"She said that my dad, Timothy Brogan, was in love with her and willing to take responsibility for her child. She told him her baby's father was dead. As far as I know, she never told him the truth. Neither of them ever hinted at it to me."

"Until she was dying and forced to leave you an orphan," Aaron said.

Brogan grunted derisively. "I'm hardly an orphan.

I have my own life, my career, and my independence. I don't need a parent. I had two. They're gone, but that doesn't leave me needy.''

Aaron had his doubts, but he wasn't going to argue the point with a grown man. ''Would you be willing to have some blood tests?''

Tyler frowned. ''I really don't see the point.''

''I'd consider it a tremendous favor,'' Aaron said. ''You might not want or need a father, but I'd like to know if I sired a son.''

Under similar circumstances, Tyler would want the truth, too. He agreed to the blood tests.

ONE

Tyler Brogan strode through the elegant foyer of Cameron Industries without a glance at the people occupying the ground floor. He headed straight for the elevator like a man with a mission, unconcerned by the many sets of eyes that lingered on his tall, handsome form.

He drew eyes everywhere he went. It used to bother him, but his experience in the corporate world had taught him to ignore the unwanted attention. He'd never understood the curiosity anyway. He was just another man in an expensive business suit.

What he didn't realize was the infinite appeal of his aristocratic carriage: striking features, wide shoulders, and lean, athletic form. He was a man with the kind of magnetic energy that would always attract attention while keeping the onlooker wary, yet fascinated.

Ty entered the elevator and punched the button for

the top floor. Then he waited impatiently to be deposited at Aaron Cameron's reception area.

"Mr. Cameron, Mr. Brogan is here to see you." Mildred Mason was mature, polished, and professional, but even she spared Tyler Brogan more than a passing glance.

Aaron glanced at his watch. It was exactly one o'clock. "Send him right in, Ms. Mason."

He rose from his chair as the other man entered his office and extended a hand in greeting over the top of his desk. Their handshake was firm but brief.

Tyler had stayed overnight in Chicago at Cameron's request. Blood tests had been quickly and discreetly arranged. The call at his hotel last night to confirm their relationship hadn't really surprised him.

Aaron hadn't been surprised, either, not after hearing Tyler's story. He had a son. He'd spent a long, sleepless night battling a multitude of conflicting emotions: fury at being denied his son, self-disgust for not being aware of Sarah's plight, and a slow-dawning jubilation at her parting gift of love.

"As I told you last night, the tests were conclusive. You're my son."

Tyler nodded, but didn't say anything. He wanted to hear what Cameron had on his mind.

"Do you have any siblings?" Aaron asked. He remembered Sarah had loved children and wanted a big family. He felt sure she'd sent her son to him for protective reasons, but he knew that Tyler wouldn't appreciate the idea.

"I have two brothers and a sister. They're all single and living at our family home in California."

"You're all close?" Aaron prodded. He didn't like

to think that his son had suffered the life of an outcast in his own home.

Ty's three siblings shared a special relationship and many friends, but he'd never belonged to their elite crowd.

"Yes, we're close, but I've never had the same interests as my brothers and sister. I live alone, travel a lot, and don't see them much anymore."

Aaron nodded in understanding. Brogan was a loner. He could empathize. His own scientific thirst for knowledge and restless energy had driven him as a young man and left him little time for socializing.

It was almost too much to absorb. He had a son, and his son was strong, intelligent, self-assured. Yesterday he'd wondered if Tyler was trying some kind of scam to gain money or power, but the younger man's attitude wasn't the least bit ingratiating. He didn't seem at all pleased with the idea of having him for a father.

"Before I came to Chicago to find you," Tyler told him in a low, even tone, "I did some checking."

Aaron smiled slightly. His son was blatantly honest.

"You have a daughter," Ty continued tersely. "I guess I have a half-sister that I didn't know existed."

For the first time since their initial meeting, Aaron's expression became shuttered, and he studied Ty with a calculating intensity that would have unnerved a lesser man.

Was Tyler Brogan utterly trustworthy? Dare he share his most guarded secret? If he didn't, his newly found son would doubtlessly create havoc with his questions. If Brogan tried to ferret out his own answers, the results could be devastating.

Aaron didn't know what the other man intended to do with the knowledge of their relationship. "My daughter's name is Chantel." That much he probably knew. "She's several years younger than you, but she's not your sister."

"How can that be?" Ty asked grimly.

Aaron's expression was equally grim. He had never discussed the circumstances surrounding Chantel's birth.

They stared at each other until Ty finally broke the tense silence. "If I am your biological son and Chantel's not my sister, then she can't be your daughter."

Aaron remained mute on the subject, trying to decide whether or not he could trust his judgment in such an important matter. Was Brogan as honest and straightforward as he seemed? What was the best way to handle the situation?

"I have to know."

Ty's hard, flat statement was the deciding factor. Chantel was twenty-eight and no one had ever questioned her parentage. An investigation of any sort could only stir up trouble and heartache. It would also pose questions he didn't want asked or answered.

"I guess there's a secret you'll have to know," Aaron ground out roughly. "But I want your word of honor that you'll never repeat what I'm about to tell you."

Intrigued, yet wary, Ty wondered if he could handle any more secrets. He wasn't anxious to take on more emotional baggage. He chose to stall.

"How do you know my word can be trusted? You're a powerful and wealthy man. I could use your secrets for blackmail."

"Sometimes a man has to make a judgment strictly on gut instinct," Aaron declared, feeling ridiculously pleased when Brogan's eyes glinted with respect.

"Can I trust you if you give me your word?" he asked the younger man.

"You can trust me."

"And I have your word that you'll never repeat what I'm going to tell you?"

Ty was growing more intrigued. "You have my word."

Aaron sighed heavily, running a hand through his hair as he tried to formulate words to describe this bizarre twist of fate. He'd never told another living soul the truth about Chantel, but Tyler was his son and deserved some explanation for a lifetime of neglect.

"When I was discharged from the army, I went to California to find your mother. You would have been about two then," he added distantly.

"I asked some mutual friends about her and learned that she was happily married, had one child, and one on the way. I couldn't believe it after what we'd shared, but it never occurred to me that her child might have been mine. We were always so careful. It just never occurred to me."

Aaron's eyes were slightly apologetic as they met Ty's. "If I hadn't been so hardheaded, I would have found the courage to confront Sarah. But she'd wounded my ego, and I tried to pretend it didn't matter."

"I headed home to Illinois and swore I'd forget she ever existed. It took me a while, but I found another woman who captured my heart. She was a petite redhead named Caroline, and I fell hopelessly in love. She had a baby daughter whom she'd chosen to raise herself, and she didn't want anything to do with men."

"To make a long story short, I eventually convinced her to marry me and let me adopt Chantel.

"My name was legally added to Chantel's birth certificate. Her natural father wanted nothing to do with her. Now he is dead, and I love Chantel more than my life. I wouldn't hesitate to destroy anyone who deliberately hurt her."

For the first time during their interview, Ty got a glimpse of the steel he knew existed beneath the calm exterior of Aaron Cameron. Chantel was obviously his Achilles heel.

"So you took the responsibility for another man's child," Ty declared, trying to make sense of it all.

"In actuality, yes," Aaron declared. "In my heart she never belonged to anyone but me from the first time I rocked her in my arms."

"A bizarre coincidence," said Ty.

"I suppose," Aaron conceded. "On the other hand, I'm sure there are thousands of men who take on that sort of responsibility every day—women, too. What's important is the kind of parent you become."

Ty watched Aaron intently, and despite his own emotional upheaval, he felt his respect for his biological father increasing with every minute.

The feeling was mutual for Aaron. He hadn't helped raise his son, but he was pleased at the results of his upbringing. He owed Timothy Brogan a debt of gratitude he could never repay.

"You never had any other children?" Ty asked. He knew Cameron was a widower with one daughter, but he was surprised by an unexpected desire to learn more about his natural father.

"We tried, but Caroline had difficulties with several pregnancies, and her health was at risk. Chantel became our world and then my sanity when Caroline died a few years ago."

Ty nodded in understanding. The loss of his parents had left him emotionally bruised and battered. Sometimes he wished for someone special to help him through the rough adjustment. His siblings had each other, but he'd never been close to any of them, and he had very few real friends.

"Can you stay in Chicago for a while?" Aaron asked. He wanted time to get to know his son.

"No. I have an evening flight back to L.A."

Aaron frowned. "I wish you could stay and meet Chantel."

"How would you introduce me?" Ty asked derisively. "If you tell her I'm your long lost son, she'll assume that she's my sister."

Aaron hadn't considered Chantel's reaction to Ty. His eyes darkened with regret as he realized that he could never share this wonderful news with her. She'd always wanted a brother, but it wouldn't be fair to let her believe Ty was related by blood.

He never intended to tell her the truth about her birth, and there didn't seem to be a feasible alternative. He would have to think of a way to overcome the apparent obstacle to a friendship between the two of them.

"I could always introduce you as a business associate," Aaron suggested. Chantel was a wonderful hostess and often helped him entertain visiting businessmen.

"Does your daughter work for Cameron Industries?" asked Ty. He was curious about her despite a gut instinct that warned him not to get involved.

"I wish I could say yes to that," Aaron replied. "She's top executive material and could easily take control of the firm, but she doesn't care much for the business."

He grimaced and continued. "Chantel insists she's a people-oriented person. She likes dealing with human beings rather than electronic devices: her words not mine. She runs her own successful, financial investment agency. She won't even do that work for me. She concentrates on service for individuals rather than corporations."

"Sounds like she has a mind of her own," Ty commented.

"That she does, and her customers trust her implicitly," Aaron added.

Ty's brows rose. "That's quite an accomplishment."

"You don't think it's wise to trust the people you do business with?" asked Aaron, noting Ty's cynical expression.

"I think it's imperative, but trust doesn't come easily or unconditionally."

Aaron agreed, but he'd had years to surround himself with people he could trust, and he'd earned their loyalty. His son might not be so fortunate.

"What's your specialty?" He'd already learned that Tyler Brogan was a respected name in Silicon Valley.

Ty's mouth twisted into a half-smile. "Microchips. My company is one of your suppliers." And Aaron Cameron's name was nationally renowned in the computer world.

"What position do you hold?"

"I'm being considered for a vice-presidency. That's why I can't afford to take much personal time right now."

Ty rose from his chair, considering their conversation at an end. He wasn't a man who indulged in small talk very often, and he'd learned what he needed to know. He couldn't afford time for private matters.

Aaron nodded, rising to his feet and offering his hand while his features took on a calculating gleam.

"If you have some tough competition for the position, you might benefit from a father who's well-known in the business."

Ty went rigid with anger and dropped the older man's hand. He didn't appreciate the suggestion. "I'm not going to tell anyone, and I rather you didn't either. I can pull my own weight," he clipped. "The only thing I really wanted from you was a denial. I wanted to hear you swear that my mother was mistaken."

"I can't give you that," Aaron said, his tone softening with respect for the proud man who had his blood flowing through his veins.

Tyler closed his eyes tightly against a wealth of emotion. Aaron had been testing him. He couldn't blame him, yet the test was a waste of time. His heavy sigh was a rare expression of fatigue.

"I have to go."

Aaron moved around his desk and walked toward the door with Ty. "I know this couldn't have been easy for you, but I'm glad Sarah sent you to me."

"Yet you're not willing to tell your daughter the truth about her parentage," Ty declared, sympathizing with Chantel because she might have to learn the truth the same painful way he had. He felt an unaccustomed empathy with her.

Aaron stiffened. "The situation is entirely different. Her father wanted nothing to do with her and made that blatantly clear. He died more than ten years ago without ever laying eyes on her, and there's no family for her to trace even if she wanted to."

"I don't imagine she'd want to," Ty said, offering his hand for another firm shake. "But I know from experience that it's not something you want to learn while you're grieving for a loved one."

Aaron's features hardened into what Chantel teasingly described as his bulldog expression.

"It's a secret I intend to carry to my grave."

Ty nodded, neither condoning nor condemning. "Thank you for seeing me." He hesitated only fractionally before handing Aaron a business card with his address and telephone number.

"If you're ever in California with some spare time, feel free to call me."

It was an unexpected offer of acceptance that momentarily shook Aaron's control. "I'd like that."

Tyler's smile was brief but sincere, and then he left without another word.

Aaron moved back to his desk and dropped into his chair feeling very old and tired. He had a son, a big, strong, intelligent son with enough courage and integrity to make any man proud.

A slow smile curved his lips and then a huge grin. He had a son. His son didn't want much to do with him right now, but that was understandable. It would take Ty some time to come to terms with what he'd recently learned.

Aaron had no intention of letting him walk out of his life now that he'd walked in. He'd already missed more than thirty years of Ty's lifetime. He fully intended to share the next thirty or so, even if he could never publicly proclaim their relationship.

There was no need for Tyler to be a threat to Chantel. In fact, it might be marvelous if the two of them met and became friends. It wasn't an impossible situation.

TWO

"No, no, no, no, no!" Chantel's brilliant blue eyes flashed at her father in annoyance. "I can't even believe you're asking!"

"It's important," Aaron told his beloved daughter.

"The man grunts, Daddy," she argued. Her silk skirt swished about her legs as she paced his office floor. "The few times I've spoken to your new protégé, he's merely grunted. I'm sure he doesn't like me at all."

Aaron smothered a grin. "I'm not asking you to have a blazing affair with him or win his undying love. I just want you to help ease him into your circle of friends."

"My friends are my friends because I don't abuse their friendship," she countered, perching on his desk and crossing her long, elegant legs.

Aaron gave her an admonishing frown. "Tyler's not that disagreeable."

24

It was Chantel's turn to give the admonishing frown. "You know he's totally hopeless. Otherwise, you wouldn't be asking for my help."

"No one is totally hopeless," Aaron taunted gently. "How many times have you dragged home seemingly worthless human beings and insisted that they were basically good, decent people who needed understanding and compassion?"

Chantel mumbled something that sounded like "petard" and tossed her heavy mane of red hair over her shoulder. She swung around on his desk to face him.

Aaron's eyes scoured her lovely features. She was gifted with a magnetic personality and generosity of heart that had often made him worry, yet she had never made him anything but proud.

"I think Ty's slightly unsociable behavior stems from basic insecurity. The move to Chicago was a complete change of lifestyle for him. He's just cautious about throwing himself into a new social scene."

Chantel snorted indelicately. "He's arrogant, and he has no desire to make friends. He strikes me as a man who is totally content with his own company."

"Yes, but you admitted that you don't really know him. I think he's just a little shy."

Chantel's eyes widened in disbelief. She could hardly believe what she was hearing. There wasn't anything shy about Tyler Brogan. The man was big, handsome, and totally self-confident.

"He's downright unfriendly," she insisted. "Every time I get near him he sends out these little signals to discourage me from getting closer."

"Little signals?" Aaron challenged.

"When he's near, my sensory antenna pick up hostile vibrations," said Chantel, dramatizing her words by lowering her voice and running her hands up and down her arms. "All the little nerve endings in my body go on alert, and the man causes me physical discomfort. My body and I know when we encounter blatant dislike. He might disguise his aversion to me, but my antenna recognizes pure male antagonism."

Aaron was shaking his head and laughing by the time she'd finished her short performance. She was delightful and so easy to love. He adored her, even when she was being obstinate and uncompromising.

His little girl had grown into an enchanting woman whose warm heart and vibrant personality captivated everyone she met. Her friends vied for her time and attention. She kept them enslaved with her keen sense of humor and fierce loyalty. Those were the traits he was trying to prey on at the moment.

"I think your reaction is a bit exaggerated, daughter."

"I'm not teasing, father," she pretended to growl, but the sparkle in her eyes belied her tone. She loved to hear his laughter and see the glow of pride in his eyes. "Brogan makes the hair on my neck rise and little quivers of alarm shiver over my body. My keen instincts of survival scream for me to run, run, run, whenever that man gets near."

Aaron's eyes suddenly narrowed in frustration. "I want Tyler to take control of this company some day, but I want more than that. I want him to become an integral part of our lives, so that he doesn't get restless and decide to move back to California."

"Why?" Chantel was genuinely curious. She'd never known her father to be so concerned about keeping an associate happy, and he'd never asked for her help.

"You have dozens of resumés from the nation's finest executives," she reminded him while absently pleating her skirt with her fingers.

When he'd let it be known that he was looking for someone to eventually take his place as CEO of the company, applications had come from all over the country.

He'd spent months readings resumés. Then he had hired Tyler Brogan as his executive assistant.

"What made you decide Brogan was the best?"

"You're the best," Aaron teased lightly with love shining from his eyes. "But you refused me, and Tyler's the next best."

Chantel felt an almost unbearable swelling of love in her heart. Whenever she felt slightly guilty about not being the son every man seemed to want, her dad assured her that he admired her just as she was.

"Thank you for that," she said softly, grasping one of his big hands and squeezing it tightly. She dearly loved this man who always encouraged her to do her own thing, even if that meant she would never take over the reins of his precious business.

"But don't think flattery will soften my stance on this insane suggestion of yours."

Two pairs of shrewdly intelligent eyes locked in mutual respect, but neither gave a hint of weakening resolve.

"I want you to befriend a lonely man. God knows

it isn't an unusual task for you. Is that so much to ask?"

It wasn't really much to ask, given her caring nature and habit of adopting strays. She'd do almost anything for her father, but the nature of his request was worrisome.

"Daddy," Chantel sighed, "the man really avoids me like the plague. How can I possibly help him when he doesn't want help? I'd appear disgustingly brazen, and I can't very well ask him to take me out. He's bound to be suspicious if I begin to take an interest in him."

"I don't want you to chase him," Aaron explained. "I just want you to make a genuine effort to get acquainted. Then you can slowly introduce him to your friends." It seemed the perfect solution to him.

"And what if he makes it painfully clear that he wants nothing to do with me or my friends?"

"You just keep trying. I know he's not an easy man to get close to, but I've never seen you fail before. You can handle it."

Chantel rolled her eyes heavenward, but she grinned at his unshakable confidence in her. If he'd asked her to do anything else she wouldn't have hesitated, but Tyler Brogan triggered an uncomfortable feminine wariness.

"You are a charming and persuasive man, my father, but this time neither charm, nor flattery, nor paternal devotion can override my intuitive objections. I do my best to avoid men like Brogan. Throwing myself at his mercy just doesn't appeal."

"What if I sweeten the deal a bit?"

Chantel caught her breath, and she eyed him as though he'd grown horns. "You're going to offer me a bribe?" she asked in amazement.

"I want you to realize how serious I am about making Tyler feel at home in Chicago. Right now he's enjoying the challenge of a new position, but he might decide to relocate if he doesn't find more here than just another job."

"Sounds unreliable to me."

"Just a man who thrives on challenge."

"And you think he'll appreciate my invasion of his private life? Don't you think a man like that would prefer to make his own way?"

"I don't want you to make it easy for him or go overboard with your attention," Aaron told her. "Just allow him to know what a wonderful person you are and let him do the rest."

"What if he isn't interested in wonderful persons?" Chantel suggested irritably. "He strikes me as a man who likes his women cold and hard."

Aaron sighed in exasperation. Then he resorted to bribery. "You know that youth center you've been begging me to sponsor?"

Chantel went stiff with surprise. He was really going to try to bribe her. "You said you were already at the limit of charity you could afford."

Aaron didn't argue, but he clarified his intentions. "If you help me with Tyler, I'll write them a check for fifty thousand dollars."

Chantel's mouth dropped open, and her eyes widened with shock. "Right now? This very week?" She knew the center for pregnant teens was in serious financial trouble. She'd been working with them for

months, trying to stretch their funds with investments, but there just weren't enough funds.

"Today, if you give me your promise."

She was sorely tempted. The money was desperately needed, but her father's motives troubled her
even more. She hated succumbing to bribery even if
she wouldn't personally benefit.

A knock at the office door kept her from immediately committing herself. She twisted on the desk to
see who was brave enough to interrupt their shared
lunch hour.

At Aaron's bidding, Tyler Brogan entered the
room, saw Chantel, and hesitated. He didn't miss the
determined glint in Aaron's eyes nor the chagrin on
Chantel's lovely features. Nor did he miss the way
she stiffened at his entrance.

"I can come back later," he declared, wanting no
involvement in what appeared to be a squabble between father and daughter.

Brogan's features lacked any expression, and it
drove Chantel crazy. It was impossible to read his
thoughts or determine what made the man tick. Normally she studied men to the point of learning their
every strength and weakness.

Usually the weaknesses outweighed the strengths
and kept her from becoming too involved. This man
refused to be pigeonholed and ignored.

"No need to leave. We've finished lunch and almost finished our discussion. Chantel can be trusted
with any information concerning the company. Did
you verify the facts and figures of the Stanforth
deal?"

"Yes."

Chantel noticed there was no subservient "sir" tacked on to his response. Her father hated subservience and obviously Brogan did, too. They were two men, much alike, but Chantel couldn't imagine herself ever being comfortable with the younger man.

"I should be leaving," she attempted.

"Sit still," Aaron commanded. "We aren't finished."

"Yes, father," she obeyed prettily, folding her hands and placing them in her lap like a proper little lady. She knew her submissive tone and actions would amuse her dad.

Aaron shot her a warning glance.

"May I have permission to stand?" she continued in a polite, meek tone. "My legs are getting little pins and needles from sitting on this hard old desk." And she didn't like the feel of Brogan's dark eyes behind her.

Aaron gave her a reluctant grin and offered her a hand as she slid to the floor. "Incorrigible brat," he accused affectionately, then turned back to Tyler.

"Do you think Stanforth is offering us a fair deal?"

Tyler moved to the desk and handed Aaron the file. Dressed in a three piece suit, shirt and tie, he made Chantel think of a wolf in sheep's clothing. She had no desire to become his next challenging prey.

His voice was low and firm and sent shivers along her nerve endings. She moved a respectable distance from her father's desk but kept watchful eyes on the men.

"I think he could improve the deal considerably. He's trying to make a fortune. His product is the best, but his price could come down a lot more and everyone would still profit handsomely.''

Aaron nodded. ''How do you want to handle it?'' He was testing again. He didn't look up from the file, but he knew Chantel was surprised by his question. He'd never let any other man make major decisions.

Tyler was getting used to Aaron's methods and didn't resent them. ''I'd tell him to negotiate in good faith or peddle his product elsewhere.'' The response was immediate and firm.

Aaron agreed. ''Do that,'' he said, closing the file and handing it back to Tyler.

''He'll want to verify with you.''

''No, he won't. I've already told him that your word is as good as mine.''

The room was suddenly, startlingly quiet. No one even seemed to be breathing. Tyler and Chantel were stunned by Aaron's bold declaration. Tyler was being trained to take over the company, but he'd only been here for three months. Neither of them had expected Aaron to give him so much power so soon.

For the first time since meeting Brogan, Chantel actually saw emotion in his eyes. Once she'd recovered from the shock of her father's words, her gaze had swung to the younger man and caught a myriad of emotion in the depths of his dark eyes. The strength of those emotions caused a faint trembling within her.

She knew she'd be wise to avoid learning any more about Brogan's emotional depths. She always tried to avoid men with a hidden wealth of powerful, passionate emotions. It was so much safer.

"Thánk you," Tyler told Aaron. "I appreciate your confidence, but if it's all the same to you, I'd prefer your approval on all major decisions for a while."

Another shock for Chantel. The man actually shared a warm smile with her father. *Good grief, he might be devastating if he smiled too often*, she thought.

Aaron gave his son a broad wink. "I'm planning on being around for a few more years. I'm just tired of the same old business routine."

"I haven't begun to tire," Tyler responded with a slashing grin that expressed his hunger for challenge.

Aaron laughed and then swung his gaze to Chantel. He supposed she had a barrage of questions for him, but he decided to forestall the interrogation.

"My daughter, Ms. Chicago Socialite, has agreed to have dinner with me tonight. How would you like to join us at my house? You're probably getting tired of cooking for yourself, and I can promise you won't find better fare anywhere in the city."

Chantel was amazed by how rapidly Tyler's defenses were repositioned.

"I don't want to intrude."

He didn't want to come, and they all knew it.

"I've been wanting to show you my private lab and get your impressions on my latest project." Aaron knew the most tantalizing ways to get what he wanted. "If you let me provide your dinner it won't seem like I'm asking you to work after hours or stealing too much of your personal time."

It was a ruse, but an excellent one, Chantel conceded. Her father was a master manipulator. She gave him a grin, then realized Tyler's bold, dark gaze was leveled directly at her.

"You won't mind the intrusion?"

Chantel wondered if he realized he'd become a bone of contention between her and her father.

"Heavens, no," she lied a bit breathlessly, having acquired a great deal of her father's diplomatic prowess. "At least he'll make an effort at polite conversation if we have company. When he has my total attention, all he wants to talk about is robots."

"You wound me, daughter," Aaron chided. "For your information, Tyler happens to be very interested in robotics."

Chantel groaned theatrically, then tried to summon a genuine smile for the younger man. "In that case, you're in for a real treat tonight," she told him.

"It's settled, then," Aaron declared in satisfaction. It had taken months to lure his son to the Cameron family home. "Chantel says she'll try to make it by six, but there's always a last minute emergency that makes her late, so we'll plan to eat at seven. You can come whenever you're free."

Tyler nodded in agreement. Then he grunted a farewell and left the room in three long strides. Chantel was sure the man had no desire to linger in her presence.

She slowly walked back to her father's desk, collecting her coat and handbag on the way. "I have to get back to the office." She leaned down to plant a kiss on his cheek, then headed for the door. "I'll see you this evening."

"Chantel," the seriousness of Aaron's tone halted her as she grasped the doorknob.

"Yes?" Her tone was just a bit cool. She didn't like being manipulated, even slightly.

"One hundred thousand a year to the center for as long as this firm is in good financial standing."

Her breath caught in her throat. Her compliance could save a lot of pain and suffering. "That's a lot of money." It would ensure the continuance and quality of service to the youth center. She couldn't refuse his bribe even though she resented it.

"I want genuine participation on your part. I'm not asking you to do anything immoral, underhanded, or out of character. Just make a sincere attempt to befriend Tyler."

Chantel didn't know why the idea of befriending Tyler made her so wary, but she couldn't let one lone man prevent her from providing a desperately needed community service.

"We have a deal," she declared, her eyes meeting his with a touch of defiance. "I will make a genuine effort, but I will not guarantee success. I don't want your contributions based on the success of a project that's practically doomed to failure at the onset."

"I understand and agree on the charity. I'll take care of the details myself. You just stop thinking so negatively."

Chantel's smile resembled a grimace. "I might be honor-bound to do my best, but I won't vow optimism."

Aaron chuckled. "I have faith in you. I'll see you tonight."

"Goodbye for now," she said as she softly closed the door between them.

Sitting back in his chair, Aaron contemplated the

scene that had just transpired in his office. Chantel was right. Sparks had certainly flown between the two of them. They had had three months to get acquainted, yet they seemed determined to keep a safe distance between them. Aaron realized that he was anxious to get Chantel's personal opinion of Tyler.

It was nearly a year since Tyler had come here to share his secret. It had taken nine months to woo the boy to Chicago, but he wanted some way to guarantee that he stayed. Chantel was his best hope.

It bothered him that he couldn't give his son the family name and that Tyler wouldn't want it if offered, but there were a lot of other things he could give. Wealth, power, prestige, and a healthy chunk of Cameron property could eventually be transferred to his son. He could also give him another family. He wanted Tyler and Chantel to get to know one another better. All he had to do was make them realize how much they had in common. It wasn't such an easy task when dealing with two strong-willed individuals.

THREE

Tyler drove his late model sedan up the long, winding driveway of the Cameron estate. Curiosity had brought him past the front gates once, but he hadn't entered the drive or approached the house.

He couldn't help being impressed by the size and grandeur of Aaron's stately home. The three-story house was built of smooth, weathered stone and surrounded by a wealth of natural landscaping that created the perfect setting for the sprawling mansion.

Aaron had encouraged Ty to visit his ancestral home, but he hadn't been too anxious to comply. Despite the proof of his parentage, Ty didn't feel any differently about his upbringing or heritage. He could cut his own path in the world and create his own heritage.

After parking the car, Tyler tightened the knot in his tie and pulled his jacket on as he walked toward the house. Aaron had been tantalizing him with frequent mentions of his laboratory, and Ty couldn't deny his interest.

He'd always had a scientific mind with an insatiable curiosity about electronics. That was one of the reasons his family could never relate to him. He'd often been dubbed the oddball because his interests and pastimes had been foreign to the rest of them.

This reminded him that he had to share the evening with Chantel if he wanted to get a glimpse of Aaron's lab. She would fit into the Brogan family like a pea in a pod. His brothers and sister were all friendly, gregarious people who shared her flair for socializing.

Ty grimaced at the thought and rang the doorbell. Maybe he'd get lucky and she'd cancel for the evening. She hadn't been any more thrilled by Aaron's invitation than he had. The two of them recognized incompatibility when they experienced it.

Aaron was the one who refused to accept the fact that his adopted daughter and biological son weren't going to become bosom buddies. They were total opposites. Maybe a few aborted attempts at congeniality would convince his dad to give it a rest.

Ty frowned at the direction of his thoughts. He didn't want to get in the habit of thinking about Aaron as his father, even in the privacy of his thoughts. It was senseless and risky.

His scowl was the first thing Chantel saw when she opened the door to Brogan. It wasn't a very good omen for the evening to come.

She summoned her best smile even though she was tired and in no mood to entertain her dad's reluctant guest. "Good evening, Mr. Brogan, please come in."

Chantel was sure he grunted his hello, but she tried to ignore him as she moved out of his way.

Ty caught a whiff of her perfume the instant he stepped through the door. She smelled sweetly feminine, but he reminded himself to ignore any masculine reaction. The Chantels of the world didn't fit into his lifestyle.

"I'm sorry Daddy isn't here to greet you, Mr. Brogan. His housekeeper, Mrs. Morley, said he would join us as soon as possible. He must have lost track of time. That's not an unusual occurrence when he's at home," Chantel explained as she led the way to the living room.

Even though Brogan kept a respectable distance between them, she was much too aware of his proximity. The fine hairs on her arms and neck were tingling with irritation.

"Can I get you something to drink?" she asked.

Ty gave the room's elegant, but homey decor a quick perusal, then turned his attention to Chantel. He wondered why she seemed so small tonight, then realized that she was barefoot. Her high heels had been abandoned beside the sofa.

Chantel felt an unwelcome blush steal over her cheeks and cursed her fair complexion. She'd forgotten her shoes and felt strangely vulnerable as Brogan's eyes moved from her discarded heels to her bare feet.

She regretted exposing any small part of herself to his dark, probing gaze. He was far too observant. He didn't say a word, but his silence was unnerving. What was keeping her dad?

"Does Aaron stock any whiskey?" Ty asked.

For an instant, Chantel wondered what he was talking about. Then she remembered she'd offered him a drink. Her blush deepened, and she silently berated her father for orchestrating this twosome. She knew he'd done it on purpose, and she swore vengeance on him for it.

"I'm sure I can find some," she told Brogan, turning quickly toward the bar to conceal her agitation. She didn't want him to realize how easily he disconcerted her.

"Daddy has a good friend who visits from Canada. His name is Ted Larkin and Mrs. Morley usually keeps some of Ted's favorite whiskey in the house. I only tasted it once and wasn't impressed, but I have their assurance that it's the best money can buy."

She was chattering like an idiot. She was used to making small talk to help people relax and feel welcome, but she was rarely reduced to nervous chatter. Brogan made her restless and jumpy. She didn't like it one bit.

Her fingers trembled when she poured his whiskey. Sheer willpower steadied her hand as she passed him a drink, being careful not to make physical contact.

Brogan's thank you sounded suspiciously like another grunt to Chantel. She poured herself a glass of wine and took a healthy swallow before turning her attention back to her father's guest.

"Please have a seat and make yourself comfortable," she urged while easing herself into her favorite chair. "If Daddy hasn't put in an appearance by

7:30, we'll eat without him. I'm too hungry to be polite for long.''

Ty sat down opposite her and glanced at his watch. It was a quarter past seven. He was starving and hoped Chantel couldn't hear his stomach rumbling in protest.

She wished she could think of something to say. Rarely at a loss for words, she was annoyed that Brogan made her feel so inadequate. She'd have to rely on her most sophisticated facade.

"Tell me about yourself, Mr. Brogan," she insisted in a voice totally lacking warmth. "Daddy says you lived in California most of your life. How is Chicago comparing? Do you have any regrets about making the move?"

Ty allowed his eyes to rest on Chantel's lovely features for the first time since entering the house. Despite the cool indifference of her tone, her eyes were sparkling with heated challenge.

He wasn't sure what he'd done to upset her, but she was definitely annoyed with him. Her eyes were bright and beautiful in the Madonna-like perfection of her face.

It was the first time in their acquaintance that Ty had seen any sign of the temper that redheads were notorious for. He was momentarily tempted to find out what made her tick, but swiftly stifled the urge. Aaron's daughter was off limits. The less he learned about her, the better.

"Well?" Chantel taunted. She didn't appreciate his intense scrutiny, and the spark of interest he'd quickly extinguished was even more unsettling than his probing eyes. His lack of response to her questions was just plain rude.

"Well what?" Ty queried softly. He allowed himself a small grin at her expense. He had an unfortunate knack for annoying even the most seasoned hostess.

"Well nothing," Chantel snapped ungraciously and drained her wine glass. The hell with entertaining her father's new assistant.

The room grew uncomfortably quiet.

Chantel closed her eyes and leaned her head back on the chair cushion. She was tired. She'd had a long day, and she didn't really care what Brogan thought of her manners.

Ty thought she was wise not to force a conversation between the two of them. They had nothing in common, yet he enjoyed the unexpected opportunity to study her.

Her mass of red-gold curls fell just over her shoulders and was gorgeous. The thick tresses were a perfect frame for her small, oval face and heavily lashed, wide-set eyes. Her skin looked as smooth as porcelain; her nose was small, and her lips were full and bow-shaped.

The blue silk of Chantel's dress suited her well. She had probably been raised in silk, satin, and lace, thought Ty. The soft fabric looked like it had been made to embrace her slender, shapely figure.

She was one beautiful woman. The stirring of attraction was hard to ignore. Normally, he'd have welcomed a chance to spend time with such a beautiful woman. Ty regretted the fact that he had to alienate Aaron's daughter. He was curious about her, but under the circumstances, any relationship between them could only lead to disaster.

Chantel was very much aware of his perusal. She could feel the heat of his eyes skimming over her features with silent intensity. Her whole body grew warm, and she was greatly relieved when Aaron finally made an appearance.

She was prepared to scold her father for his neglect, but one glance at him drained her annoyance. His hair was sticking out in every direction, his shirt was rumpled, and his bifocals were askew on his face.

He'd obviously been working in his lab, and his radical change from high-powered executive to absentminded professor always delighted her.

"You forgot us, didn't you?" she chided.

"No, no, of course not. I just lost track of time for a few minutes," Aaron explained, running his fingers through his hair in an effort to smooth it.

"Until your stomach started growling?" Ty asked with a knowing grin. He was equally amused by the change in his host.

Aaron chuckled. "I knew you'd understand. Chantel's not quite so forgiving."

"I've been stood up more often," she teased, rising from her chair. "Can we eat now?"

"Certainly," agreed Aaron. "I told Mrs. Morley to serve dinner. I hope you and Ty have had a chance to get to know one another a little better."

Chantel didn't even spare Brogan a glance as she accepted her father's arm. She didn't care if he found his way to the dining room or not. "We've been chatting like old friends," she lied without remorse.

Aaron took his usual seat at the end of the table. Chantel sat to his right with Ty on his left. Mrs. Morley had them all served within minutes of being seated. Since they were hungry, they ate in silence until the worst of their hunger was satisfied.

When Ty's hunger had abated somewhat, he directed his attention to Aaron. He couldn't get over the change in a man he'd never seen with a hair out of place. Gone was the immaculate business suit, silk shirt, and tie. Gone was the air of sophistication.

The president of Cameron Industries looked like he'd been caught in a whirlwind. Ty grinned because he knew Aaron didn't care how he looked. He obviously had more important things on his mind.

"I take it you've been working on an electronics project," Ty said, breaking the amiable silence.

Aaron nodded. "I'm working on some program chips for my robot. The whole project is coming along nicely, but I still have a few bugs to work out."

"Did you build the robot yourself?" asked Ty. He'd given the idea some thought, but never seemed to find the time.

Aaron nodded again and finished his meal. Then he gave Ty a brief description of how he'd constructed his robot.

Chantel had heard the details many times. Her dad gave her regular updates on his project, but she didn't have much of a mind for electronics. She could see that Brogan was just the opposite. He appeared to understand everything her dad was saying. He also seemed genuinely interested in Aaron's project.

"I call my robot Chan, which is short for Chantel," Aaron told Ty with a teasing glance at his daughter. "She insisted that the robot have a name, so I used part of hers. That makes her its godmother, I imagine."

Chantel groaned in disagreement, but returned his teasing banter. "You couldn't keep calling your prize possession 'that robot thing,' " she argued, "even if it is just a hunk of metal and wires."

It was Aaron's turn to groan. "I get no respect," he grumbled. "I'm on the verge of an electronic miracle, and she calls my masterpiece a hunk of junk."

Ty grinned again and was surprised at how much he enjoyed their lighthearted exchange. There was no doubt that father and daughter adored one another.

"What is the purpose of your project?" he asked.

Chantel tried to hide her grin behind her glass. This question always prompted her father to become very vague. Even though he was full of enthusiasm for his work, he carefully guarded the details of his project.

"I'm creating a multi-programmed, hypersensitive security robot to be used as a night watchman for office buildings and warehouses," Aaron explained without hesitation. "I've already programmed it to secure a perimeter with regular movements, but now I'm developing an artificial sensory system that will react to abnormal sounds, odors, or changes in moisture and temperature."

Chantel stared at her dad in amazement. She knew his plans for the robot, but she'd never heard him whisper a word of description about it to anyone else.

She slowly placed her glass on the table. Then she shifted her eyes from Aaron to Brogan, back to Aaron and back to Brogan. His avid interest in her dad's project wasn't faked. He had the same gleam in his eyes that her dad always got when he discussed anything electrical in nature.

"So the robot will be more than a guard against intruders," said Ty. "It will also guard against water or fire damage."

"Exactly," Aaron agreed. "Some buildings suffer more damage from smoke, fire, or malfunctioning sprinkler systems. The robot is equipped with an alarm system that would alert officials to the same kind of problems a human would notice, and there would be no threat of physical harm."

Chantel couldn't believe her ears. Her dad was sharing information that he'd kept confidential for nearly a decade. She knew he trusted Brogan when it came to the business, but now she was forced to re-evaluate the other man's importance in her father's personal life.

How well did her dad really know Tyler Brogan? How carefully had he investigated Brogan's past? Why was he so eager to share the details of his experiments with a veritable stranger? Had she missed some important piece of information about Brogan that explained her dad's absolute faith in him?

Maybe Brogan was another electronic genius, thought Chantel. Perhaps her father recognized a kindred spirit in the younger man. They both seemed to be totally engrossed in the details and calculations of the robot project.

Normally when Aaron started spouting off electronic equations, his guests got that glassy look in their eyes that denoted total confusion. Brogan's eyes were alight with enthusiasm and comprehension.

Chantel could only hope that Brogan wouldn't betray Aaron's trust. She would personally see that he was drawn and quartered, then tarred and feathered, if he dared to hurt or disappoint her father.

"What about unexpected entries into a building by people who work there?" Ty asked Aaron.

"That would be set up by a fingerprint scan," the older man explained. "Only one entry door could be used after business hours, and the robot would have a file of fingerprints to identify anyone passing through the doors."

Aaron halted his discussion while Mrs. Morley cleared the table and poured coffee. Then Tyler questioned him about the robot's mobility, and he explained in more detail.

"The robot will be programmed with coordinates for the north, south, west, and east sections of any building where it's used. Every quarter hour it will move from one coordinate to another."

"Couldn't a burglar watch the pattern of the robot's movements and break into the building when the robot is farthest from the entry point?" asked Chantel.

Both men looked at her as though they'd totally forgotten her existence. It wasn't a very complimentary reaction, but her dad immediately included her in the discussion.

"I've taken that problem into consideration," supplied Aaron. "The robot won't have a regular pattern of movements."

"If it's programmed in advance, how can it not have a regular pattern?" Ty wanted to know.

"I've created a series of movements that are based on random numbering. Something similar to a lottery. Each spin of the wheel punches up a different combination of coordinate numbers. The same series of coordinates might not be repeated for weeks or even months."

Chantel was always amazed at her dad's genius for problem-solving. Tonight was no exception, and for the next hour he explained his solution to every question or probable concern that she and Brogan could anticipate.

The conversation drifted over Chantel's head when the men talked about specific calculations and programming, but she found herself caught up in their enthusiasm.

"If Cameron Industries ever markets this robot of yours," she put in toward the end of a lengthy discussion, "you shouldn't have any trouble with your sales pitch."

Aaron chuckled and gave her a broad wink. "By then you and Ty will have all the pertinent information. I'll let you two handle the sales."

"Oh, no, you won't," countered Chantel, shaking her head in disagreement. "I am not in the electronics business and never plan to be. You'll have to depend on Mr. Brogan for marketing skills."

"Mr. Brogan's name is Tyler," Aaron teased her. "Since there's just the three of us here, I think he'll forgive a lapse in social graces and allow us to speak on a first name basis. Won't you, Ty?"

Chantel had noticed that Brogan wasn't too pleased

by her dad's mention of her working for Cameron Industries, but his frown was replaced by a bland expression when Aaron directed his question at him.

"Ms. Cameron is welcomed to use my first name," he replied, his eyes glinting with challenge.

Aaron laughed happily. "Chantel, meet Tyler. Ty, meet Chantel. Do you think the two of you can relax your guard long enough for a stroll to my laboratory?"

Chantel was trying to think of a way to excuse herself from their little stroll when the telephone rang. Mrs. Morley brought a portable phone to the table.

"It's for you, Mr. Cameron. It's George Hanley, and he said it was important."

Aaron grumbled but accepted the telephone.

Chantel and the housekeeper exchanged a grin. Everyone who telephoned Aaron insisted that his call was important. Margaret Morley had been working for the Camerons nearly twenty years, and she'd become adept at screening calls.

"More coffee?" Mrs. Morley asked quietly.

Chantel and Tyler both shook their heads.

"Why don't you call it a night," Chantel whispered to the housekeeper so she wouldn't distract her dad from his conversation. "I'll take care of everything," she added, knowing that Margaret was addicted to prime time television. She hated to keep her working so late.

The housekeeper smiled and nodded. "Thanks, there're just the coffeepot and cups that need rinsing. Have a good evening," she added quietly.

"You, too," said Chantel. Then she watched Margaret leave the room so that her eyes wouldn't drift across the table to Brogan.

Aaron concluded his call and put the phone down with a sigh. "George says they think Harry Murdock has suffered a heart attack. It doesn't appear to be too severe, but I really should go to the hospital."

Chantel's eyes immediately reflected concern. George and Harry were poker buddies of her dad's and had been great friends to him since her mother's death.

"When did it happen? Is he going to be all right?"

"About four this afternoon. George says he's in stable condition now, but they don't know how much damage was done. They're allowing visitors for a short time this evening. I'd better get cleaned up and go."

"Do you want me to go with you?" asked Chantel.

"No, that's not necessary," Aaron insisted. "I'd rather you stay here and show Ty my lab. I've been promising him a grand tour for weeks, and I hate to put him off."

"That's no problem," argued Ty. He wasn't anxious to spend the rest of the evening alone with Chantel. "I can come again when you have more time."

"I'm sure you'd give a much better tour than I could," Chantel added. Brogan's swift rejection of her dad's suggestion irritated her, but she shared his distaste for being thrust at each other.

"Please?" Aaron gave her his rare, coaxing smile, and Chantel's resolve wavered. She hated being manipulated again, but she knew he was really worried about his friend. There was no reason to add to his concern.

"Okay, I'll play tour guide," she agreed on a sigh. "But I can't promise to do it nearly as well as you could."

The relief on Aaron's face was a fitting reward for her efforts. He gave her a swift kiss as he rose from his seat, then turned to Brogan.

"Ty, I hate to run out on you, but Harry's a good friend. Chantel knows a whole lot more about my lab work than she lets on. Any questions she can't answer, I'll be happy to answer later."

"Don't worry about it," said Ty.

Aaron gave them both a smile and left the table. "I'll lock the front of the house when I leave, Chantel," he said over his shoulder as he exited the dining room.

An immediate, heavy silence fell over the room. Ty and Chantel stared warily at each other across the table.

"I can see the lab some other time," he repeated.

Chantel shook her head slowly. "I told him I would show you the lab, so I will." But she didn't make any move to rise from her chair.

"Then I'll help clear the table," said Ty. He rose, grabbed the coffeepot and his cup. "Didn't you promise Mrs. Morley to finish the dishes?"

Chantel nodded and collected the other dirty cups, then led the way to the kitchen. The dishes were cleaned and the room tidied in a few short minutes. They worked together in near silence, but the tension between them was steadily increasing.

When they were finished, Chantel led Ty through

a short hallway that connected the back of the house to Aaron's lab. She was extremely aware of him. All the nerve endings in her body remained on high alert due to Brogan's proximity. They refused to relax and give her a respite.

The large building they entered had originally been built as a four-car garage. Her dad had converted it to a lab. It was divided into two rooms; the smaller one was used as an office, and the larger one housed Aaron's laboratory equipment.

Chantel stopped at the door and punched in an access code to enter the lab. The electronic panel clicked like the cylinders of a safe, and then she heard the heavy lock being released.

"Did your dad design his own security system for the house and lab?" asked Ty.

Chantel had already learned that Brogan didn't waste time on small talk, so she assumed he was really interested.

"If you haven't realized by now," she said lightly, "my dad is a wizard when it comes to electronics. He wouldn't dream of letting anyone else handle his security."

Brogan didn't respond, but she could almost feel his smile, and that unnerved her. She quickly flipped every light switch on the wall panel. Aaron's lab was immediately illuminated.

It always reminded Chantel of a set for *Star Trek*. Computer systems were everywhere. Despite Aaron's occasional lapses in forgetfulness, he was never lax about the cleaning and upkeep of his equipment. Everything was made of the finest quality, was kept in excellent repair, and shone from constant use and care.

Chantel tried to tactfully put some distance between her and Brogan by crossing the room toward a closet where Chan the robot was stored. Then she turned to see his reaction to her dad's favorite playroom.

Brogan's eyes were alight with awe and appreciation. Chantel groaned inwardly. He looked just like her dad when he got that gleam in his eye. She feared she was in for a long, boring evening.

Ty could hardly believe his eyes. There was a fortune in equipment housed in the lab. He knew a few research scientists who would sell their souls for the opportunity to work in a lab like this. No wonder Aaron was so proud, yet secretive about his work here.

Chantel watched him moving around the room and studying everything with fascination. Her sigh was heartfelt. Brogan really was as bad as her father. She might as well have been a doormat.

FOUR

"Would you like to meet Chan?" she finally asked, just to regain Brogan's attention for a minute. She was more than a little piqued at how quickly he'd forgotten her existence.

Ty forced his eyes from an especially interesting computer system. He could tell that his hostess was annoyed again. For some reason her indignation appealed to his sense of humor.

"Chan the robot?" he dared to tease.

Chantel nodded and told herself that she wasn't the least bit affected by the devilish gleam in his eyes or his teasing tone. It was her dad's equipment that had improved his mood, not her.

She punched another security code into the panel on the closet. The door slid aside, revealing a collection of bright chrome robots, all in various forms of construction. The one her father had named Chan was the only finished product.

Chantel stepped aside and waved her hand in an all-encompassing gesture. "Look to your heart's content," she invited.

Ty had already moved closer and hunched down to study the robot. Chantel shook her head in resignation and hoisted herself onto a workbench where she could sit while he played with Chan.

The robot was about three feet tall and covered with switch panels. Chantel had always thought it looked like a shiny fire hydrant with glandular problems.

"Which switch turns on the main power?" asked Ty.

"The one behind his left ear," Chantel explained in a tone filled with wry amusement. Her dad hadn't given Chan ears, eyes, and a nose, but the robot had plenty of knobs and buttons as substitutes.

Ty frowned, then reached to the left of the top portion of the robot. He flipped a switch and heard the whirring of several computer programs spinning to readiness. Chan began to speak through a recorded voice system.

"Chantel. Chantel. I smell Chantel."

Chantel and Ty shared a look of surprise. Then she groaned in exasperation. "What has my father done now?"

With an increase in the whirring noise, the robot turned and moved slowly toward the bench where Chantel was sitting. Ty stepped out of the robot's path.

"I think Chan's looking for you," he suggested with a slashing grin.

She didn't care for the way his grin made her heart

flutter. Brogan could prove to be a very dangerous man if he smiled too much.

"Chantel. Chantel. I smell Chantel." The robot droned insistently. It stopped a few inches from the workbench and lifted two metal appendages that served as arms.

Ty chuckled at Chantel's grimace of displeasure.

"Hug, hug, kiss, kiss, my little namesake."

The robot's chant drew a heartfelt moan from Chantel. Hot color swept over her cheeks, and she flashed an irritated glance in Brogan's direction. He looked ready to explode.

"Hug, hug, kiss, kiss, my little namesake," repeated the robot, stretching its appendages straight up to Chantel.

Ty's amusement couldn't be contained any longer. He knew he was adding insult to injury, but he roared with laughter. The sight of the robot lifting its mechanical arms and chiming hug, hug, kiss, kiss was more than he could handle.

Chantel glared at Brogan, then the robot. "I'll get even for this, Aaron Cameron," she swore to her absent father. "And you can be disassembled, you mimicking mound of metal," she threatened as she jumped down from her perch and quickly flipped off the robot's power.

Ty's arms were crossed over his stomach, and he was laughing so hard that he could barely catch his breath. The robot's programmed antics were outrageous enough, but Chantel's wounded dignity, her flare of temper, and useless threats brought on another round of laughter.

The object of his amusement crossed her arms over

her chest and kept glaring at him. She knew her annoyance added to his enjoyment of the situation, so she decided to issue warning.

"You think it's so funny, Brogan?" she challenged. "Just wait until my father programs his mechanical midget to identify your scent. Just wait until it asks you for a kiss and hug. I hope it happens in a boardroom filled with executives!"

Ty had been trying to control his laughter, but her dark warnings fueled it more.

Chantel's annoyance was quick to fade. She felt as though she were watching the unveiling of a beautiful portrait. Brogan's laughter burst through the carefully constructed layers of sophistication and hardened businessman facade. It gave her a peek inside his person to the very real, very appealing Tyler Brogan.

She knew intuitively that a glimpse of the man inside the executive was dangerous, yet it was so tempting. If she weren't careful, the real man might invade and delight the secret part of herself that she never shared with anyone.

When he began to get control again, she barraged him with more warnings. "Believe me, Brogan, your time's coming, and then we'll see how hysterically funny you find the situation. Hug, hug, kiss, kiss," she mimicked the robot's mechanical tones.

"Stop!" Ty finally found his voice and begged her to give it a rest. He straightened, swiped the tears from his eyes, and tried to drag in a calming breath.

Chantel was grinning mischievously. Her little fits of temper rarely lasted long, and she could never resist a man with a wicked sense of humor.

Brogan's eyes sparkled as they locked with hers.

For just an instant she witnessed a glimmer of the same kind of helpless fascination she was beginning to feel. Her stomach muscles tightened in response. She didn't want to be intrigued by a big man whose whole demeanor shouted sex appeal. She was determined to keep their relationship platonic.

"Better now?" she asked, forcing a light tone.

Ty nodded, but waited another minute before trusting his voice. "I'd like to know how Aaron did that."

"The sensory device?" asked Chantel.

Ty nodded again, finally tore his eyes from her, and concentrated on the robot. "Did he have it programmed to play that recording anytime the power is on or only when your scent was identified?"

"I'm not sure," Chantel replied. "But if he asks for a sample of your favorite cologne, I'd advise you to refuse."

Ty fought off more laughter. She was really getting to him, and he'd promised himself to stay completely immune to her charms. He knew she could wrap her father and lots of other men around her little finger, and he didn't care to be part of that crowd.

"How often does the power pack have to be regenerated?" asked Tyler, changing the subject. He was careful not to look at Chantel. She was already close enough to tantalize him with her scent.

"Daddy made his own tiny generator. It continually recharges the robot's batteries. Everything will eventually wear out, but not as often as a regular power pack."

Ty turned his head to see if she was being serious.

The unexpected movement caught Chantel off guard. Their faces were suddenly just inches apart. Their eyes locked. Their breathing seemed to falter.

She retreated first and put a safer distance between them before responding to the question he hadn't even voiced.

"I'm thoroughly convinced that there's nothing my father can't do if he puts his mind to it. His only drawback is a shortage of time. I've begged him to sell the company and devote himself to his research."

Time and money had always been Ty's drawbacks. There never seemed to be enough of either, but he didn't allow himself the luxury of regret.

"Has Aaron listened to your advice? Is he considering selling the company?" he asked. "I know he's anxious to retire."

Chantel sighed and began to pace around the room. "I wish he would consider it, but until he hired you, he was bullheaded about keeping the business in the family. I had finally convinced him that I would never want it, but I think he was still holding out a hope that I'd marry someone who would want it."

"And there was no chance of that?" asked Ty. He was tinkering with the robot but giving Chantel his full attention.

"No way," came her emphatic reply. "I love my father, but I will never marry a carbon copy of him. I'd prefer a man who wants to come home at night, one that wants me more than he wants the wealth and power of success."

"Sounds boring."

The remark was so matter-of-fact that Chantel didn't take offense, but she did give the idea some thought. Every time she believed she'd found a man who best suited her needs, she ended up bored. Maybe there was some truth in Brogan's casual comment.

"Do you plan to marry a woman who's a business asset, or would you prefer a wife that really wants to be with you?"

Ty considered the question for a minute. He had no intention of marrying in the near future, if ever, but high on his list of priorities for a wife was a woman who didn't drool over his brothers when he took her to meet his family. He'd never met a woman who could pass the family test.

"That question sure brought a frown and some deep contemplation," remarked Chantel.

"I'm not planning to marry, so I hadn't given the subject much thought," Ty responded. "But I think I can survive the corporate jungle without leaning on a woman."

"I suppose you're one of those people who thinks they don't need emotional support from anyone," she challenged.

"You asked about a business asset," he countered, his eyes still focused on the robot.

"And you suggested that an asset meant someone you could lean on," argued Chantel. "Leaning on someone means accepting their support," she continued. "That suggests you really want someone more concerned about you as a man rather than as Brogan the Executive."

"The two are indivisible." His reply was succinct. He didn't want Miss Socialite delving into his psyche.

Chantel might have agreed a couple hours ago. Now she wasn't so sure. The brief glimpses of the man behind the facade had been intriguing. Maybe there was some hope of reforming him. She had to try; she'd promised her father.

"I'm having a little get together at my apartment tomorrow night," she declared before she could lose her nerve. "Would you like to join us?"

Ty straightened to his full height and gave her his total attention again.

"Why?" he asked, eyes narrowed.

Chantel hated the warmth that flooded her cheeks. "I thought you might like to meet some of my friends. You haven't had much time to socialize since you came to Chicago. Daddy says you work too much."

"Did Daddy suggest you invite me?" asked Tyler.

Chantel lowered her lashes to block out the intensity of his sharp gaze. She briefly debated about her response. Brogan wasn't a fool. He knew she wasn't anxious to spend more time with him. The truth seemed safest.

"Actually, Daddy offered me a bribe I couldn't refuse," she explained, looking him straight in the eyes when she dropped her bomb.

Ty's eyes narrowed and his lips thinned. Aaron's manipulations didn't surprise him, but Chantel's complicity both surprised and disappointed. It infuriated him that he felt any reaction. He leaned against a workbench and crossed his arms over his chest. His eyes were leveled at Chantel. "Want to explain?"

Chantel's eyes were cool. She didn't like his defensive attitude. She wasn't any happier about the situation than he was. "Well . . ." she drawled, "Daddy insisted that I didn't have to do anything illegal or immoral."

"That's a relief," clipped Ty. "What exactly did you agree to do?" He realized that the thought of her trying to seduce him held more appeal than he cared to admit.

"Daddy is determined to see that you're happy and well adjusted. He wants me to introduce you to friends and ensure that you feel welcome and comfortable in Chicago."

"How the hell does he expect you to do that?"

"That's exactly what I asked him," Chantel retorted, her tone as grim as his. "He must think I'm a magician with a magic wand."

Ty fought a grin. She wasn't any happier about Aaron's interfering than he was. "If I don't cooperate, and you can't do anything illegal or immoral, then what?" he asked.

He was teasing her. Chantel felt the little flutterings of excitement again. She copied his stance by leaning against a workbench opposite him and crossing her arms over her chest. The look she gave him was daring.

"I may have to resort to bribery myself," she explained. "But first I have to find your Achilles heel."

"I don't have one. What's yours?" he shot back swiftly. He knew she didn't want anything from Cameron Industries, and Aaron said her investment business earned a healthy income. So how had she been bribed?

Chantel shrugged, not sure she wanted him to know any of her weaknesses.

"A new car, furs, jewels, your very own golf course?" he taunted, determined to drag the information from her. "If I'm the object of this bribe, I should at least know how high the stakes are."

Chantel's eyes were flashing with fire again. She'd never accepted any kind of bribe before, and her compliance in any matter couldn't be bought with material possessions. She gave him the truth, but not all of it.

"I've been promised a hundred thousand dollars a year for as long as Cameron Industries is financially sound," she taunted back at him, making it sound as though she was taking a cash payment for her services.

Relief washed over Tyler, then annoyance at the rush of reaction. He didn't like unexpected emotional rushes.

Aaron had explained the company's contribution to the teen pregnancy center. He hadn't explained that he'd used the donation as a bribe. Ty understood Chantel's reason for accepting the bribe, but not Aaron's reason for making it.

"A hundred thousand a year is a pretty hefty payment for services that aren't illegal or immoral," he pointed out mockingly. "What does Aaron expect to buy for his money?"

Chantel was aggravated by his arrogant tone and attitude. She didn't like his deliberate emphasis on the word "services." "He wants me to ensure your happiness and see that you never want to leave Chicago."

"How the hell are you supposed to do that?"

"You tell me."

"What if you fail?"

"Payment is not contingent on success."

Ty whistled softly. He was flattered by Aaron's determination. He'd made the bribe virtually irresistible. Chantel's charity would benefit even if no one else did.

He didn't plan to leave Cameron Industries for any reason short of death, but he was intrigued by the fact that Aaron believed Chantel could affect his decision. The man certainly had confidence in his daughter's abilities.

"How are you supposed to earn your money?" Ty asked, his eyes gleaming devilishly as he returned her steady gaze. "I'm curious as to how Aaron thinks you can keep me happy."

Chantel didn't blink an eye. She couldn't believe he found the situation entertaining, but she wasn't going to let him use it to his advantage. She knew he wasn't thrilled about spending time with her.

"I'm supposed to introduce you to my friends and the benefits of living in Chicago. Daddy's sure you'll be happy and content once you become comfortable socially."

Ty didn't bat an eye or say a word, but he allowed himself a stream of silent curses. If there was anything he didn't want, it was to be sociable, especially with Chantel's crowd. He didn't want his name on any social registers, and he didn't want to be bombarded with invitations that he wouldn't accept.

Chantel allowed herself a grin. "I get the impression that you aren't pleased by my father's latest attempts at manipulation.''

Ty's frown deepened. She was getting a kick out of his displeasure. Well, he had some bad news for her.

"Did your dad tell you why I left California?"

"No. I assumed it was because he made an offer you couldn't refuse. He's very good at that.''

Ty decided to be as honest and straightforward with her as she'd been with him. "I was being considered for the vice-presidency of the company I was working for. If I'd gotten the promotion, I wouldn't have moved for any amount of money.''

Chantel wasn't really surprised by the admission, and she didn't question the truth of his statement. She doubted if the money meant half as much to him as the power.

"You didn't get the promotion?"

Ty explained, his tone echoing his disgust. "The board of directors decided they wanted a vice-president who could double as a public relations man. My competition had all the social skills, so he got the job.

"I was assured that I had the highest qualifications, the necessary skills, and best work record for upper level management, so they gave me the honor of carrying the work load while the official vice president socialized.''

Chantel hated discrimination of any kind. She could understand his frustration. "That stinks," she commiserated.

"I thought so." Tyler agreed. He also liked the

way her eyes flashed at the injustice. "When Aaron offered me a position here, I took it."

"So why is he afraid you won't stay?" asked Chantel. She abandoned her defensive stance and took a seat on the workbench again. "Would you go back to California if someone offered a more powerful position?"

"No." There was no hesitancy in Ty's response. Their eyes met, sizing each other up again.

"You sound very sure."

"I'm positive."

"Being CEO at Cameron is important to you?"

"Very."

"And Daddy knows that?"

"Without a doubt."

"Then why did he bribe me to keep you happy?"

"I have no idea."

That wasn't quite the truth. Ty understood why Aaron wanted them to get to know each other. He just didn't think it was such a good idea.

Surely her dad wasn't matchmaking! The possibility hit Chantel like a ton of bricks. She stared at Brogan in consternation. She hadn't given it much thought before now because Aaron had never interfered with her personal life.

He'd never tried to bribe her before, either. She guessed that anything was possible, but she was still a little stunned to think that her dad believed she and Brogan would make a good match. Maybe he still hadn't give up hope of keeping Cameron Industries in the family.

"What grim thought brought on that frown?" asked Ty.

"I've told him that I could never be serious about any man who worked for Cameron Industries," Chantel explained. "But he thinks he knows me better than I know myself. He thinks I'll put up with his matchmaking."

"Matchmaking?" Ty didn't think Aaron actually wanted a romantic match. It was clear to Ty that he wanted them to care for each other, although he wasn't willing to tell Chantel the truth about their parentage. Obviously, Ty could hardly explain that to Chantel, though.

"I've told him I don't want the company, and that I have no intention of marrying anyone who wants the company," explained Chantel as she jumped from her perch and began to pace. Her tone grew more agitated as she continued.

"Now he's decided you're the best man for the company, so he wants to kill two birds with one stone. He wants you to have both his company and his daughter!"

Ty knew she was wrong, but he didn't know what he could say to her. Aaron had certainly been pressuring them to get better acquainted. He decided to downplay the idea.

"That would make me the stone." Ty tried to distract her with his teasing.

"What?" Chantel was confused for a minute, then remembered her two birds with one stone cliché. She couldn't help grinning at the comparison. Imagining him as a stone and herself as a bird tickled her funny bone.

"I'm not sure I like being a bird," she said with

a chuckle. "I wouldn't mind the flying, but I don't want to eat bugs or be killed by stones."

Tyler was fascinated by the way her temper flared so easily then was swiftly doused by her lively sense of humor. He grinned at her. "I don't think I like being dead weight."

Chantel laughed, but the laughter got caught in her throat when she looked into his dark eyes. He really was a threat to her composure when his smile reached the depths of those sable brown eyes. She could learn to like it too much.

"So what do we do to convince him he's wrong?"

"Ignore him?" suggested Ty.

"That won't work with Daddy. He's one of the most persistent men I've ever met, and he can be such a nag."

"What do you suggest?" Ty asked, suspecting that she was already formulating a plan.

"You could just cooperate," Chantel suggested.

"You want to get married to stop your father from nagging?" he asked in genuine amazement.

"No!" Damn her fair skin and the constant blushing. "I mean go to a few parties, date a few of my friends, and try to enjoy the social scene. If you hate it, you can ease back into isolation and tell my dad that you're happier that way. If we don't make any effort at all, he won't concede defeat."

Tyler supposed she was right, but he didn't want to be exhibited like a visiting jock.

Chantel didn't like the scowl on his face. She tried coaxing. "It's for a good cause."

"The teen center?" he asked absently, his mind

still on the pitfalls of spending too much time with Chantel.

"How did you know about that?" she asked, propping her hands on her hips and glaring at him again. "Have you been playing dumb the whole time I was trying to level with you?"

She was one gorgeous woman, thought Tyler. Few women had ever challenged him so relentlessly. "Aaron explained that the company would be setting up a fund for the center. When you told me the exact amount of his bribe, I put two and two together."

Chantel relaxed and grinned. Brogan was good at lighting her fuse even when he wasn't trying. She decided they'd better be partners. Maybe if she spent more time with him, the fascination would wane. It usually did.

"So are you coming to my party?" she asked when he started to turn his attention back to the robot.

"How formal is it?" Tyler was hedging while he considered the options and possible consequences. Parties weren't his favorite pastime. He wheeled the robot back to the closet.

"It's very informal. This is no sophisticated social event, just some of my friends and their friends."

"Do I need a date?"

"No."

"How many unattached women will be there?"

Chantel couldn't tell if he wanted more or less. She decided he probably wouldn't like the role of most eligible bachelor. "There will be a few, but I'll protect you from them if you like."

Ty frowned at her challenging expression. The

only woman he needed to avoid right now was her. Still, she had the most logical solution to the problem. Aaron wouldn't be satisfied until they got to know each other better.

"What time?"

FIVE

The party started at eight. Ty arrived early so that he could check out the guests as they came. He thought it better to know what he was up against before being thrown into the middle of it.

He wore brown slacks and a matching brown turtleneck with a tan sports jacket. It was the first time Chantel had ever seen him without a suit and tie. Her pulse skipped a beat or two, but she blamed it on her hurried state.

"Make yourself at home," she told Brogan after their initial greeting. She waved toward the living room.

Her apartment was big and spacious. It was decorated in earth tones, but there were splashes of bright color everywhere. Ty thought it a perfect setting for her.

"I have a few things to finish if you'll excuse me for a minute," said Chantel, already heading for the kitchen.

"Anything I can help with?" asked Ty as he followed her, taking in every detail of her appearance.

She was wearing emerald green stirrup pants with a clinging, multicolored sweater that reached her thighs. Her hair was loose and cloaked her shoulders, left partially bare by the wide neckline of her sweater. She looked soft and sexy.

Ty briefly wondered how she would feel in his arms. The urge to find out was swiftly controlled. He'd let his guard down last night, but he couldn't risk letting it happen too often. Women like Chantel Cameron were a menace to a man's peace of mind.

"If you really don't mind," said Chantel, "you can help me carry some of these hors d'oeuvre trays into the living room."

Ty eyed the trays of cheese and crackers, finger sandwiches, and vegetables with dip. He'd worked late and was starving. Nothing he saw looked promising.

"Have you had dinner?" Chantel asked with a grin. He had the look of a hungry man.

"No."

"There's chicken and ham in the refrigerator. The bread's in a drawer by the sink. Help yourself."

She got a slashing grin for her efforts. It did crazy things to her insides.

"I'll help with the trays, first," Ty told her as he picked up two and carried them to the living room. "Where do you want them?"

Chantel was following with another tray. "I cleared some space on the coffee table. You can put those two there." She had a portable bar and a small dining room table where more food could be placed.

"Can I fix you something to drink?"

"Not on an empty stomach, thanks. I think I'll raid your refrigerator if you really don't mind."

"I really don't mind," she teased.

Ty went back to the kitchen, and Chantel made some last minute adjustments in the living room. She turned the stereo on at a low volume and dimmed some of the lights.

She quickly checked her bedroom and the bathroom for any personal items that hadn't been put away. Then she ran a brush through her hair and applied some lip gloss.

Brogan's early arrival had caught her by surprise. She hadn't been sure that he'd come, and she was annoyed at how pleased she'd been to see him. Besides being gorgeous, he made her feel heady with excitement. Then she dismissed those thoughts and attributed the strange feelings to the anticipation of her party.

She rarely entertained at her apartment. Even though she loved to socialize, she loved her privacy more. The only time she invited friends to her home was when she felt guilty about not inviting them for so long.

She wondered how everyone would react to Brogan. He wasn't a party animal, of that she was certain. He'd probably be bored stiff, but there was little she could do to prevent it. If they wanted her dad to stop hassling them, then they had to prove there was no match to be made.

The doorbell rang, and Chantel headed to the living room. Ty was coming out of the kitchen. "Did you ward off the hunger?" she teased.

"For the time being," came his succinct reply.

Chantel opened the door to Don and Jeanette Menter. Jeanette had been her college roommate, and the two of them remained good friends. Don and Jeanette had lived together for five years but had recently married.

"The newlyweds!" Chantel teased, ushering them in the door and making introductions to Brogan. She'd decided to introduce him as an executive with Cameron. Her closer friends would be curious, but she could explain later.

"I brought food, and Don has wine," said Jeanette. "Where do you want it?"

"Wine to the bar, food to the dining room," instructed Chantel as she helped them with their coats.

"Where are you putting the coats?" asked Tyler as he took the burden from her arms.

"You can lay them on my bed," she said. She hadn't planned on putting him to work, but playing host would help keep him occupied. "That way," she added, pointing to a door leading off the living room.

Guests were arriving off and on for the next hour. Chantel was kept busy with introductions and greetings. Brogan didn't have much to say, but he helped a lot, and they made a good team.

Everyone knew that Chantel avoided men who worked for Cameron Industries. She wasn't sure if Brogan was aware of all the silent speculation, but she was as aware of her friends' curiosity as she was of the man himself.

It was after nine o'clock before they had another minute to themselves. "Is this everyone you're expecting?'' Ty asked, dipping his head close to hers so he couldn't be overheard.

Chantel stood in the dining area and swept the living room with her eyes. More than a dozen people were enjoying the food and visiting with one another. Besides Don and Jeanette, there were two other married couples, an engaged couple, two single women, and three single men.

''I'd say this is the bulk of the group,'' she replied.

''Quite a collection,'' he noted.

Chantel grinned. Her friends were a wild mixture of personalities. ''Do you remember everybody's names?''

Ty cocked a brow in response, and she chuckled.

''I'm sure they'll all reintroduce themselves sometime during the evening,'' she assured him.

''You mean they'll all want a chance to grill me about our relationship.''

Chantel laughed lightly. ''We don't have a relationship. But they don't know that, so I'm sure they'll have questions. Just watch out for Lester, the aging hippie. He reads minds.''

Ty grimaced. ''I could go tend the bar,'' he suggested. ''That's the customary place for meaningful discussions.''

''Do you know anything about bartending?'' Chantel felt compelled to ask.

''That's how I worked my way through college.''

Chantel wasn't surprised. She could easily imagine him working in a bar. He probably hadn't been too free with advice, but she could see him filling in as a bouncer.

"What are the artists' names?" asked Ty, his attention directed toward Chantel's guests.

"Joe and Ellen Simpson. They're both very talented."

"Who'd you say the Don Johnson look-alike was?"

She hid a smile by leaning over the table and busying herself with a tray of food. "His name is Ken Gratton. He's a real estate agent."

"And the one who looks like Tony Danza?" asked Ty as he stole a sandwich from the tray she was straightening.

"His name is Tony, but the last name's Carbalso. He runs a restaurant here in town."

"Are they fighting over you?"

"I date them both occasionally," Chantel supplied while deciding she'd had enough of his questions. "Are you going to tend the bar?"

"Break's over, back to work?"

"You got it."

With an exaggerated sigh, Ty grabbed another sandwich and headed across the room. Chantel was immediately joined by her best friend, Shelley Harding. She and Shelley had known each other all their lives, had attended grade school, high school, and college together.

"Chan-tel," Shelley always made her name sound like a chant. "You've been standing over here grinning for a full ten minutes. I thought you didn't like your dad's new assistant. What's happening here?"

"Nothing for you to get all hyper about," Chantel told her. "I promised Daddy I would introduce Brogan to some of my friends, that's all."

"You said all he ever did was grunt."

"He has a droll sense of humor."

"Does that mean you actually find him likable?" Shelley wanted to know. She helped herself to a cracker, munching it while watching her friend.

"I don't know him that well." Chantel knew she sounded evasive. How could she make Shelley understand her rapport with Brogan when she didn't understand it herself?

"Well, he's certainly creating a stir tonight. Most everyone is curious and wants to get to know him better. Ken and Tony are so used to competing with each other for your time that you've thrown them into total confusion."

"Be nice, Shelley," came a reminder from Chantel. Her friend had never been fond of either man. In fact, she never approved of any of the men Chantel dated.

"Maybe they'll be so confused that they'll leave and never find their way back," Shelley suggested. "They're both too wimpy for you anyway."

"I like them," Chantel defended, not for the first time. "They're both nice guys."

Shelley groaned. "Nice guys come in last. All you ever date is nice, safe guys." It was a familiar lecture. "It's about time you found somebody exciting and dangerous—like Tyler Brogan."

"Oh, yeah?" Chantel clipped. "You should see him in my dad's lab. He gets that mad-scientist gleam in his eyes, just like Daddy's. Next time they're together discussing electronics, I'll invite you to join us."

Shelley groaned louder. "He can't be as bad as your dad," she insisted.

"Wanna bet?"

"But he's so sexy."

"You'd better not let Brian hear you discussing another man's sex appeal."

"Brian pulled back-to-back shifts yesterday. He's a walking zombie tonight. He wouldn't care if I crawled into Brogan's lap and gave him a hug."

Shelley's fiancé, Brian Lands, was in his last year of residency at the same hospital where Shelley worked as a registered nurse. Their conflicting schedules were always interfering with their social life.

Chantel looked toward Brian. He was tall, thin, and dark, a complete opposite to Shelley's short, plump, and blonde. They loved each other very much. Brian smiled at them, but his eyes were bloodshot from lack of sleep.

"The poor guy looks worn out," Chantel told Shelley. "Why don't you take him into my bedroom and let him get a little sleep."

"Huh!" Shelley snorted. "If I take him into your bedroom, he'll suddenly have a resurgence of energy. Sex is an amazing motivator. It never fails. Tonight I told him he can just wait until bedtime, like the rest of the world."

Chantel laughed happily and hugged her friend. Then they were joined by Misty Carter, a coworker of Chantel's. The shapely brunette was twice-divorced, loved men, and made no secret of the fact.

"I heard you guys talking about sex and decided I'd better come and get all the details. Were you discussing the hunk Chantel's been hiding? He has more than his fair share of sexual magnetism."

Chantel frowned. She'd never been bothered by Misty's references to other men, but for some reason she didn't like hearing her purring tones in relation to Brogan.

"Why don't you get some dancing started, Misty?" Chantel asked. "Ken wants to learn that new one you were showing us at the club."

"Shouldn't you start the dancing?" asked Misty.

"I'd better start circulating. Shelley, get Brian on his feet and shuffle him around the room for a while. It'll get his adrenalin pumping."

"Good idea."

The apartment had a small area near the balcony windows where dancing could be done. Misty and Ken, Brian and Shelley, and several other couples took advantage of the limited space.

Chantel made a point of spending some time with each of her guests. Then Misty started a game of partner switching. After every dance, each dancer had to find a new partner. The energetic brunette even coaxed Brogan to cooperate, but only on the slow songs.

As the evening wore on, everyone's pace began to slow, and they tuned the stereo to a station that played mostly love songs. Misty and another co-worker, Donna Evans, were making sure that Brogan changed partners with each dance. He didn't neglect his duties as bartender, but he spent most of the night with a woman in his arms.

Chantel didn't suppose he ever lacked for female attention. Her dad was crazy to think Brogan needed any help when it came to socializing. He didn't seem to have much to say to his various partners, but that didn't stop them from showering him with attention.

It was after eleven when Tyler got tired of dancing

and even more tired of dodging questions. He parked himself on a stool behind the bar, making it clear, without saying a word, that he didn't want to dance anymore. He poured himself a whiskey and watched his hostess.

Chantel had managed to keep her distance from him most of the evening. It was relatively easy because he stayed close to the bar, and she was busy replenishing the food supply or catching up on her friends' personal news. The two of them didn't dance together.

Still, she'd been aware of his eyes following her constantly. Every time she glanced at him, his eyes were on her. Tension vibrated between them, and she knew her friends were aware of the silent communications.

Chantel could hardly understand her own feelings of anticipation. She felt like she was just biding her time until everyone was gone. Normally she loved a party, but tonight she was impatient to be alone with Brogan.

It was stupid. For all she knew he might be the first to leave. *He might leave with Misty or Donna*, she argued to herself, but she really didn't believe it.

Chantel felt the need to dispel her increasing sense of excitement as the evening grew late. She decided the best way to do that was to spend some time with him and assure herself that she was mistaken about his intentions. There was absolutely nothing going on between her and Brogan.

Another slow ballad was playing. Shelley was fast asleep on the sofa, sitting in the circle of Brian's arms. Don and Jeanette had left early. Nearly every-one else was dancing. She made her way to the bar and sat on a stool beside Brogan.

"Decide to light for a while, butterfly?" he asked her, his eyes warm.

Chantel smiled. "It does feel awfully good to get off my feet."

"It's the first time you've sat down all night."

"Well, no wonder I'm dragging," she exclaimed softly.

Tyler liked the sound of her voice, the scent of her perfume, and having her beside him. He hadn't given it much thought before, but he realized Chantel was the kind of woman a man wanted to keep all to himself.

"Had any rowdy drunks at the bar yet?" she asked him.

"Misty's getting a little tipsy, but I heard Ken promise to drive her home. She should be as safe as she wants to be."

Chantel smiled. Misty always came by taxi. That way she never had to refuse a ride home or limit her drinking. "Misty has a system."

Ty's right eyebrow tilted upward. "I imagine it's foolproof. I hope you aren't too attached to Ken."

Shaking her head, Chantel took a sip of the cola she'd poured herself. Fortified, she asked, "Did you meet anyone you'd like to spend some time alone with?"

"Were you hoping I would?"

Chantel remembered the unexpected and uncom-fortable pangs of jealousy she'd experienced every time she'd seen him with another woman in his arms.

"I asked you here so that you could get to know some people."

"The bartender always gets to know everybody," he told her. "Misty's ex-husbands were too possessive. Ken's boss is a bastard. Donna's boyfriend is on the road too much and leaves her alone. Joe and Ellen have an art exhibit next week, and Tony has financial woes."

Chantel laughed softly. "I guess you were getting acquainted with everybody. What do you think of Brian and Shelley?" She glanced at the sleeping couple as she spoke their names.

Ty followed her glance. "Brian and Shelley don't get enough sleep or enough of each other."

Chantel nearly choked on her cola.

"I meant that in a purely platonic fashion," Ty explained, his eyes wicked. "Although Brian has been nibbling on her neck most of the night."

Her soft laughter made his pulse accelerate. He was finding her too easy to like. He wanted her in his arms. He wanted her all to himself.

They watched as Shelley woke up, stretched, and groaned. Then she poked Brian in the chest. He grabbed her and tried to pull her back into his arms, but she resisted.

"Come on," they heard her say. "Let's help clean up and head home."

"You don't have to do any cleaning," Chantel insisted from her seat behind the bar. "There's not that much to do."

"The doorbell's ringing," Shelley told her. Chantel couldn't hear it over the music. "Want me to get it?"

"Please."

"Expecting any late arrivals?" asked Ty.

"Nope." Chantel knew she should go to the door, but she couldn't find the energy. When she recognized the newcomer, she was glad she hadn't moved.

Her temper flared swiftly, her eyes flashed fire, and her features stiffened in anger.

Ty was quick to pick up the negative vibrations. "Who is he?"

"His name's Geoff Duncan. Geoff with a G," snapped Chantel.

"Was he invited?"

"He knows he's not welcome in my home."

"Sit tight," said Ty, rising. "I'll get rid of him."

Chantel was startled by his declaration. She put a hand on his chest to halt him and gave him a grin. "You do take your bar duties seriously, don't you?"

Ty looked down at her and smiled. The spurt of anger had vanished. Her beguiling eyes were dancing. Her hand resting on his chest was causing a riot of heated reaction throughout his body.

His hand came up to cup her face of its own volition. His thumb stroked her petal-soft cheek. "Who is this guy?"

Chantel couldn't seem to catch her breath. Brogan's touch and the heat of his eyes held her mesmerized. It was an effort to get words out. "Everybody has one big mistake in their life. Geoff's mine."

"You're not still carrying a torch?"

"Not even a little flame."

Shelley interrupted their brief moment of shared intimacy. "Chantel, guess who's here?"

Ty shifted so that he was standing behind Chantel as Geoff followed Shelley to the bar.

"I told him to keep his coat on because the party's over," declared the feisty blonde.

Geoff was blond, too, with blue-eyed, all American good looks. He was tall, well-built, and supremely confident. He refused to accept the fact that Chantel wanted nothing to do with him.

The unwelcome guest completely ignored Shelley. "Hello, Chantel." His tone was smooth as he stepped up to the bar and greeted her, giving her what she considered his come-hither smile.

"Hi, Geoff, are you lost?"

Ty forced back a grin and draped an arm around Chantel's shoulders. He was surprised to feel how tense she was, and he wondered if she'd lied about not caring for the grinning Casanova.

"I know the territory pretty well," he responded with a mocking grin, his eyes insinuating more than his words.

Chantel stiffened and felt Ty's arm tighten around her. She placed a hand lightly on his forearm and warned herself not to show any reaction to Geoff's deliberately provocative words.

"The territory is off limits to you," she responded lightly. "I'm surprised you would stoop to party crashing when I've made it perfectly clear that I don't want to see you."

Geoff's smile didn't falter. "Actually, Donna invited me to come with her, but I couldn't get free earlier." His eyes went to Ty.

"This must be the new head honcho at Cameron," he said while looking pointedly at Ty's possessive hold on Chantel. "I thought you'd sworn off electronics executives, especially anyone working for Daddy," he taunted.

Chantel felt Brogan go tense, so she rested her head back against his chest and gripped his arm tighter. She masked her swift jolt of anger with a calm smile. She wasn't about to give Geoff the pleasure of causing a scene.

"Some men are worth changing your mind for," she declared in a softly taunting tone. Her smile was smug. His eyes flared with temper, and his face suffused with color.

"Clean up time!" yelled Shelley, flipping on the overhead lights and moving to the stereo to shut off the dancing music. "Everybody get to work!"

"Shelley!" Chantel scolded. "Guests aren't supposed to help with the cleaning."

"Maybe not," she argued, "but friends are. Get the coats, Brian."

Brian shot Chantel a glance. "Bossy, isn't she?"

"Geoff, you made it!" Donna exclaimed as the music died. She abandoned Tony and came to slip an arm around Geoff's waist. Then she shot Chantel a guilty look.

"I hope you don't mind me inviting Geoff," she said hesitantly. "We've all been friends for a long time."

"You know you're always welcome to bring a guest to my home," said Chantel.

Ken and Misty joined the growing crowd around the bar. "Hi, guys," said Misty in a slightly tipsy tone. "Ken is going to take me to an all-night nightclub. You want to come with us?"

Donna began to coax Geoff to join them, and Chantel turned her attention to Shelley. "Brian, grab your woman and don't let her touch another dirty plate!"

"You heard that, woman!" Brian growled, catching Shelley around the waist and making a show of wrestling her into her coat.

Chantel laughed at their clowning and forced herself to move from her comfortable perch. Tyler stayed close to her as she assisted her guests with their coats and said her goodbyes.

Brian and Shelley were the first to leave, and the others followed in a steady stream until everyone except Brogan was gone.

Chantel closed the door with a sigh and leaned against it, facing Tyler.

He thought she looked sleepy and incredibly sexy.

SIX

"Tired?" he asked, moving closer until he could reach out and grab a handful of satin curls. His fingers had been itching to touch her hair, and he could no longer resist the urge. It felt as soft and silky as he'd expected.

"Just a little," she replied, her breathing becoming difficult with him so near. "I'm sorry if I offended you with anything I said to Geoff, but he knows how to make me see red."

"I thought you controlled your temper very well. I would have smashed his face."

Chantel laughed softly. "He isn't worth the effort."

"What did he mean with his remarks about Cameron and your dad?"

"Geoff used to work for Daddy," said Chantel, pushing herself from the door and putting some space between them as she explained. "I thought we had a promising future until Geoff learned that Daddy was looking outside the company for someone to take over the business. Geoff thought his relationship with me was a guarantee of the CEO position.

"When I told him I wouldn't try to influence my dad's decision, we had a parting of ways. Needless to say, I didn't like being used."

Chantel started gathering dirty dishes. Shelley had taken most of them to the kitchen. Ty helped with the rest.

"Did Aaron fire him?" he asked.

"No, I didn't tell Daddy the whole story. He just told Geoff that he didn't feel he had the qualifications to run the company. Geoff resigned in a fit of temper, then went to work for Andersons."

Ty whistled. "Cameron's major competitor."

"The ultimate desertion," agreed Chantel as she loaded the dishwasher.

"What's he want now? Another chance at you and the family business?"

Chantel shrugged. She didn't know what Geoff wanted. "I owe Shelley a favor for doing so much cleaning. I didn't realize how beat I was until I sat down for a few minutes."

Ty studied her delicate features. "Is that a hint for me to leave?"

Chantel gave him a wide grin. "No, it isn't."

"Good." He gave her a matching grin. "Because I've been waiting all night to dance with you."

Her breath seemed to get caught in her throat. Their eyes locked, hers wary and his determined.

"Do you really think that's a good idea?" Chantel whispered softly. The tension between them was volatile.

"Probably not," said Ty, "but I've wanted to feel you in my arms ever since I walked in the door tonight."

His admission of need struck a responsive chord in Chantel. She knew it was dangerous to play with fire, but the temptation was hard to resist. "Please don't feel obligated to console me. I don't want you to misconstrue anything I said to Geoff."

"This has nothing to do with Geoff."

It was just between the two of them. Chantel knew, but she couldn't help being wary. "It's asking for trouble," she proclaimed huskily. She'd been bribed to entertain him. He worked for her dad and was another scientific slave. They shouldn't feed the attraction.

Ty didn't say a word, but held a hand out to her. She barely hesitated before slipping her smaller hand into his large one. The heat of his grasp warmed her whole body.

He drew her into the living room, dimmed the lights, and turned on the stereo. Then he pulled her more fully into his arms, locking his hands behind her back and drawing her close.

Chantel laid her hands on his shoulders and eased the gentle curves of her body against his hard frame. "Why didn't you dance with me earlier?" she asked, tilting her face up to his.

"I didn't want to share," he responded lightly. And he hadn't wanted a room full of curious onlookers when he held her in his arms.

His eyes roved over every feature of her face like a caress. Chantel felt the warmth of his gaze reaching deep inside of her. In a few words he'd shattered any resistance she was still harboring.

As they began to sway to the music, she studied his features just as intently as he studied hers. There was strength in the hard lines of his face but incredible tenderness in his dark eyes. His lips were full and looked surprisingly kissable.

Ty had studied her from a distance for the past three months. She was everything he'd never been: charming, lighthearted, extroverted. He'd promised himself to steer clear of her. He'd had every intention of keeping that promise until she'd started arguing with Aaron's robot last night.

He couldn't remember ever laughing so hard or falling so completely under a woman's spell. He'd spent the day reminding himself of all the reasons they shouldn't become involved, but he'd come to the party, drawn despite himself.

"Did you find the party an awful strain on your patience?" Chantel asked lightly.

He didn't like crowds. He'd been impatient to be rid of her friends, but he hadn't felt uncomfortable. "Did I seem impatient?"

"No," she countered. "I thought you were a really good sport considering you didn't know anyone."

"Good sport, huh?"

"And a good bartender."

"How do you know? You didn't drink anything but diet cola."

"You seemed to keep everyone else happy. They even used your shoulder to cry on," Chantel teased, giving him a dazzling smile.

Ty forgot the conversation. He stood still and

tightened his hold on her. He wanted to kiss that smile. When Chantel smiled, the warmth seemed to come from deep in her soul and shine from her eyes. The warmth touched his soul and melted his reserve. He wanted a taste of her sweetness. His head dipped as he gently brushed his lips back and forth over the tantalizing curve of her mouth.

Chantel's breath got trapped in her throat. The hard, warm feel of his lips sent a jolt of electricity through her. She tilted her head back farther, closed her eyes, and welcomed the feel of his mouth on hers.

He didn't need any further invitation. He captured her lips with a hunger fueled by primitive male need and hours of fantasizing about the taste and feel of her.

Chantel's response was equally fierce; her lips molded themselves to the firm pressure of his mouth. They both moaned softly, and then their kiss suddenly gentled and slowed.

Ty slid his tongue into her mouth and slowly, carefully explored the moist sweetness he found. Chantel's tongue gently stroked his, and his whole body tightened at the feel of her responsiveness.

She slid her arms around his neck and stood on tiptoe to bring herself closer to his hard length. She felt the heat of his hands as he slid them to her hips and pulled her closer. The melding of their bodies created even more heat.

She offered no resistance until she felt the burgeoning strength of his arousal against her stomach. She forced herself to lean back and look Ty in the eyes. The searing heat of his gaze made her pulse flutter erratically.

"Am I shocking you?" he demanded gruffly, making no attempt to loosen his hold on her.

"A little," she replied, her tone as rough as his. "We hardly know each other."

"I know I want you."

His words stole her breath. Her eyes widened as she returned his steady gaze. "Are you sure any woman wouldn't do?" she asked. As far as she knew he hadn't been dating anyone since moving to Chicago.

"I didn't have the same reaction to Misty, or Donna, or anyone else tonight," he assured her, his hands gently kneading her spine.

Chantel was pleased with the knowledge. Misty had been giving Ty plenty of encouragement. "You did have women hanging on you all night," she charged.

"And you danced with every man at the party at least three times each," he countered, tenderly nipping at her lips. He used his tongue, his teeth, and then his tongue again to caress her mouth.

Their eyes met, and neither of them tried to hide the tumult of emotion that churned between them. Both were captives of the unexpected, but fierce attraction.

"Kiss me," Ty coaxed huskily.

Chantel didn't need to be asked twice. She stretched on tiptoe and wrapped her arms as tightly as she could around his neck. Then her lips were on his, her mouth parted, and she slipped her tongue into his mouth in search of its mate.

Ty groaned and lifted her tightly against his body. She tasted sweeter than any woman he'd ever known, she felt as though she were made for his arms, and she was all woman.

He wanted her closer. He wanted to see and touch and taste. He rocked his body against her softness, and the heaviness of his arousal throbbed between them. His blood pressure soared. Desire ripped through him, hot and heavy.

Chantel felt him shudder and realized how totally selfish she was being. She was causing him a physical discomfort that she had no intention of relieving.

"Tyler!" she breathed huskily, releasing his mouth for just the instant it took to murmur his name. Then she stole one more long, drugging kiss before forcing herself to relax the gripping hold she had on him.

Ty allowed her to withdraw just far enough so that he could scatter kisses over her face and down to the pulse throbbing erratically at her throat. He sucked gently, licked her baby soft skin, and ran his mouth back up to hers.

"You taste good," he murmured against her lips.

Chantel's heart pounded wildly. Her chest was heaving, her breasts tender and straining against the restriction of clothing. She was growing intoxicated from the erotic sensations his mouth sent coursing over her body. No man had ever made her feel so wanton and wanting. The experience was heady and a little alarming.

She had thought herself in love with Geoff, but he had never made her feel so dizzy with excitement. Brogan made her feel utterly feminine and incredibly desirable. She was fast losing control, and that was something she'd never done before in her life.

"Tyler!" Now she was begging for a respite.

He lifted his mouth from hers and looked deeply into her eyes. He saw a passion that matched his own.

"I don't suppose you're one of those totally liberated women who's willing to invite strangers into her bed," Ty whispered gruffly, leaning his forehead against hers and trying to calm his raging hormones.

The weighty resignation in his tone amused Chantel, but she slowly nodded her head, and both their heads rocked back and forth in a negative motion.

"I don't suppose you're even protected."

The negative motion was repeated.

"Damn!" he growled softly. He didn't carry that sort of protection with him, either.

He could feel the tightness of Chantel's nipples pressing against his chest. She was equally aroused. He wanted to explore every inch of her, but he didn't want to rush her or take needless risks.

Instead, he held her gently and began to dance again. She laid her head on his shoulder, and he stroked her back. He let the sweetness of her scent engulf him, and they slowly got their desire under control.

Chantel had never felt so special in her life. Being in Ty's arms was a joy like none she'd ever experienced. He was big, warm, and excitingly male, yet his tenderness made her feel cherished.

She knew all the arguments about becoming involved with a man who worked for her dad. She could tell that Brogan had reservations, too, but the attraction was stronger than the objections.

One song ended and another began. They just kept dancing. Neither of them wanted to put an end to their time together. Then a clock chimed softly, reminding them of the lateness of the hour.

"I should be going," Ty murmured against Chantel's ear, pressing kisses on the tender skin.

She shivered as goose bumps raced over her flesh. Lifting her face, she gave him a dreamy smile. "You don't have to hurry."

"You're about to fall asleep in my arms," he teased, rubbing his nose against hers.

Chantel didn't tell him how much the idea appealed. She wouldn't mind going to sleep and waking up in his arms. The intimacy of her thoughts shocked her, and she forced herself to put some distance between them.

"I guess it is getting pretty late," she said.

"You need to get some sleep."

"I suppose."

The reluctance in her tone sent a quiver of longing through Tyler. They both knew they shouldn't let their relationship progress any further, yet neither of them wanted to say goodnight.

Chantel didn't want the night to end, and she didn't want Brogan to leave. "You could stay and sleep on my sofa."

He was shaking his head before she finished the sentence. "Thanks, but it's not a good idea."

Chantel sighed in resignation, and Tyler pulled her against his side as he walked to the door. He promised himself that the next time he wouldn't leave.

"What's on your agenda for tomorrow?" he asked.

"I'm helping with some remodeling at the teen center. You're welcome to come and help me paint."

Ty grinned. "I can't make it tomorrow, but I'd like to visit the center sometime."

"The work is ongoing," she teased. "Whenever you visit, you get a paintbrush."

"How about next Sunday?"

"Are you serious?"

"I'm serious. That doesn't mean I'm good at painting, but I'm willing to help."

"Great!" said Chantel, giving him a squeeze. "We can always use two extra hands."

"It's a date, then. How about the rest of the week?"

Their eyes met and locked. He was telling her that he wanted to see her on a regular basis.

Chantel was thrilled at the prospect. "Are you just asking me because I promised Daddy I'd socialize you?"

Ty pressed a swift kiss on her lips. "No."

Her mouth widened into a smile, and she stole a longer, sweeter kiss. "In that case, I have a dinner party Wednesday, theater tickets for Friday, and I'm planning to attend Joe and Ellen's art exhibition next Saturday. You're welcome at all three."

Ty groaned. "That's not exactly what I had in mind."

Chantel laughed happily. "I'm already committed for this week, but I can promise to let you know about anything that might interest you more in coming weeks."

"I'd like that." He wanted time alone with her.

"But you'll still be my escort this week?"

His eyes told her he didn't care for her choices of entertainment. "We might as well get the socialization out of the way first."

His grudging attitude brought more laughter. "Cheer up, you might just learn to enjoy yourself."

"We'll see." Ty opened the door, gave Chantel another swift kiss, and let himself out. "Lock the door behind me. I'll call you tomorrow."

"Yes, sir," she sassed.

When the door closed, Chantel locked it and fastened her security latch. Then she turned out all the lights and headed for her bedroom.

Half an hour later, she'd taken a quick shower, donned her nightgown, and climbed into bed. She was mentally reliving the evening when the phone rang. A glance at the clock showed that it was after two.

"Hello." Her voice was drowsy as she answered the phone.

"Hi." The low, seductive tone of Tyler's voice produced a sleepy smile on Chantel's features.

"Hi, yourself," she responded, snuggling under the covers and cradling the phone against her ear. "Did you make it home safe and sound?"

"Uh huh," he said. "But I forgot to tell you thanks for inviting me to your party."

"How terribly remiss," she teased.

"I considered coming back, but I was afraid I might wake you."

"I just climbed into bed."

"Really?" His tone dropped again, his imagination running rampant.

"Really."

"Are you lonesome?"

"Just a little, but I'm used to sleeping alone."

"Glad to hear it."

The possessive quality of his voice would have made her furious with most men, but instead it gave her a wild thrill. She'd never been tolerant of possessiveness from anyone, but Brogan was different. She didn't waste time analyzing the fact.

"Are you in bed?" she asked him.

"Stretched out on top."

Chantel took a deep breath, wondering if he'd shed his clothes already. "It didn't take you long to get home."

"I only live a couple blocks away," Ty explained. He finished stripping and tossed aside the last of his clothes.

"Really?" That surprised Chantel. Apartments were hard to find in her neighborhood. "How'd you manage that?"

"I didn't, Aaron found the apartment. Did he have to pull some strings?"

"Probably," replied Chantel. "He has friends who own property in the area. He found this one for me. Don't worry. I'm sure he didn't have anyone evicted to provide us with homes."

"That's a relief."

"I'm hopelessly spoiled," she retorted. "But I do have a conscience."

Ty's husky laughter sent a quiver of awareness over her body. Chantel closed her eyes and tried to imagine what it would feel like to have his arms around her now.

"Chantel?" His tone was barely audible.

"What?"

"Would you think I'm mentally deranged if I asked if you sleep in the nude?"

Her soft laughter carried over the lines and sent a shudder through Ty. He was still one big ache. He hadn't been with a woman for months, and it had nearly killed him to leave her tonight.

"I'll answer your question on one condition," she teased.

"What's that?"

"You have to tell me first."

"Tell you what?" he asked.

"What you're wearing," she insisted.

"That's easy," he clipped. "Nothing."

His succinct reply brought a blush to Chantel's whole body. Her breasts suddenly became tight and aching.

"Your turn," Ty reminded. "What are you wearing?"

"Besides my blush?" she quipped. She could hear the devilish amusement in his reply.

"Does the thought of my nude body make you blush?" When she didn't immediately reply, he continued to tease. "If just the thought makes you warm, I wonder what would happen if you could see and touch."

"Spontaneous combustion?" she queried mischievously.

Her suggestion brought a low groan from Tyler. His body was already overheated. He tried to convince himself that the self-torture was character-building. He flipped on to his stomach to try and ease the acute ache of arousal.

"Tyler? Are you still there?"

"I'm still here, but I wish I was there."

"Do you?" she inquired softly.

"Or that you were here." His ache increased with the thought of her in his bed.

"I think we need to get to know each other a little better before we start having sleep-overs," insisted Chantel.

"I suppose," growled Ty, his tone contradictory. They were both quiet for a minute, and then Chantel spoke again.

"Do you still want to know if I sleep in the buff?"

Ty groaned again. "I don't think I can stand having you describe some silky, sexy nightwear."

"Maybe I sleep in a sweatsuit or an old t-shirt."

"That would be a criminal offense," Ty declared. Skin like hers should be draped in silk, satin, or nothing at all. He'd prefer the last.

"Actually, I'm wearing a very modest cotton nightgown," Chantel explained.

She'd never indulged in such blatant sexual banter, but she felt bold with Brogan, and she was thoroughly enjoying herself. "I could take it off if you'd like."

The deliberate taunt made Ty's blood pound through his body like a volcano rushing toward eruption. His moan was low and needy.

"You have a cruel tongue, woman," he managed to rasp into the phone. "I hope sometime soon you'll be prepared to back up those words with action. Preferably sometime when I have you all alone and can show you how much the gesture means to me.''

Chantel didn't try to contain her amusement. She laughed delightedly. The mock severity of his words didn't come off too well when he growled in such a sexy, teasing tone. She laughed sleepily until her laughter was interrupted by a wide yawn.

"Excuse me," she said.

"Am I boring you?" Ty asked. He was getting addicted to the sound of her husky laughter. He knew she was tired and that he should let her get to sleep, but he was reluctant to say goodbye.

His tone and question brought another smile to her lips. "I think you're probably the least boring man I've ever met, Tyler Brogan."

"Really?" He liked the sound of that.

"Really," she insisted. "But it's time to get off the phone and go to sleep, you know."

"I suppose," he conceded.

"Happy dreams," Chantel chanted softly.

"You, too," Ty murmured gruffly, then hung up the phone. He knew what kind of dreams he was going to have. His mind and body refused to let go of the image of a sexy redhead with dancing eyes that seared his soul and threatened to steal his heart.

_____ SEVEN _____

When Chantel walked into her own office on Monday, she felt her usual thrill of accomplishment. Her business space was only a tiny portion of a giant building complex, but she didn't mind. She was proud of her four rooms in the high rise office tower.

Donna Evans was her assistant and would soon be an active investment agent. Misty Carter handled all the secretarial duties and was incredibly efficient and dependable. The three of them had chosen the decor for their offices, and the overall effect was bright, inviting, and tastefully done.

Misty was just hanging up her coat when Chantel walked into the office. They greeted each other with smiles and good mornings.

"How was your weekend?" Chantel asked, slipping off her coat and straightening her yellow wool suit.

Misty was wearing a pale blue skirt and sweater

outfit. She started making their morning coffee. "It was okay," she said. "Thanks for a good time Saturday night."

"You're welcome. Did you go dancing until the wee hours of the morning?"

Misty moaned. "Yes, dancing and drinking. I had a rotten hangover yesterday."

"You always have rotten hangovers," Chantel reminded. "I'd think you'd get wise to what causes them."

"You know the old saying," Misty retorted, running a quick comb over her sleek, dark hair. "Old enough to know better, but too young to resist."

Chantel laughed and shook her head. Misty never seemed to tire of the swinging-singles life. She was short, petite, and packed with energy.

"I hope you don't mind my going with Ken. You said there wasn't anything special between the two of you. And your Mr. Brogan was acting pretty proprietorial."

"You think so?" asked Chantel. She'd wondered how her friends would react to having Brogan at the party.

"He never took his eyes off of you. You danced with everyone, yet Brogan managed to stake a claim without saying or doing anything in particular. I've never seen anything like it, but it sure was effective."

Chantel wasn't sure she liked the idea of having a claim staked. She hadn't realized how the interaction between her and Brogan might be conceived by her guests.

"Do you think everyone got the same impression?"

"Yep," Misty declared as she slid into the chair

behind her desk. "Ken, Geoff, Donna, and I had some weighty discussion after we left your apartment. Unfortunately, I can't remember much of it."

"Misty!" Chantel chided.

"You'll have to ask Donna. Ken and I did more dancing and drinking than gossiping. Geoff was the one who wouldn't drop the subject."

Chantel frowned. She didn't want Geoff concerning himself about her personal business.

"What I'd like to know," Misty continued, "is how you managed to get Brogan to talk. He didn't seem short on words for you, but I couldn't get much more than a few grunts out of him."

Laughing, Chantel opened the inner door to her office. "I'll have to speak to him about that grunting. It can be really annoying."

"Does that mean you'll be seeing a lot of him?" Misty wondered. "If I remember correctly, I'm supposed to knock you in the head with a large, hard object should you consider dating another man who works for Cameron Industries."

Chantel laughed. She remembered vehemently swearing off men who worked for her dad. "Brogan's different," she explained. "He's already the chosen one. Daddy plans to turn the business over to him regardless of how I feel."

"Maybe he wants to have the business, be a part of the family, and share the wealth, too," Misty suggested with genuine concern in her eyes.

Did Brogan want it all? Chantel had no way of knowing, but she understood Misty's concern. For most of her life she'd been hounded by men who thought of her as a ticket to power and wealth. Her friends knew how much she detested being used.

"I don't think Brogan's all that interested in the family wealth. He's more interested in the power, and he's earned that without any help from me. He also gets a thrill out of working with Daddy."

"He's not another electronics nut, is he?" Misty wanted to know.

Chantel's grin was self-mocking. Her friends also knew that she'd sworn off men who had the least little interest in scientific experimentation. She didn't want a man who was happy to spend his every free minute buried in a laboratory.

"He even speaks my father's language," she confessed with a resigned sigh.

"Chantel, are you crazy? This man is everything you've promised yourself to avoid! Take it from someone who knows. You don't want to be one of those women who always falls for the wrong type of guy! How can you even think about dating Tyler Brogan?"

Chantel had asked herself the same question many times over the weekend, but then she would picture Brogan's eyes as he'd danced with her and seduced her senses. She knew it was too late to call a halt to what was happening between them. Right or wrong, she was totally fascinated by the man.

"Chantel?"

The ringing of the phone put an end to their discussion.

"It's your dad," said Misty.

"I'll take it in my office," Chantel responded, moving quickly toward her desk.

"Good morning, Daddy," she said into the receiver while easing herself into the chair behind her desk.

"Good morning, Sweetheart, how was your weekend?"

"Just fine." Chantel knew he was fishing for information, and she wasn't about to supply it.

"How about having lunch with me today?"

"I'm sorry, I'm really swamped."

"Tomorrow?"

"The whole week looks like a busy one," said Chantel. Her father was going to get the brush-off for a while.

"You have to eat," Aaron growled. "If you can't come to my office, I could bring some lunch over there."

That would be a first, thought Chantel. Her dad had never made a habit of visiting her office.

"I'm afraid food will have to be sandwiched between appointments this week." Chantel said and then quickly changed the subject. "How's Harry?"

"Harry?"

"Harry Murdock, your friend," she reminded. "He suffered a heart attack Friday night."

"Oh," Aaron hesitated. "It wasn't too bad. He didn't suffer any permanent damage, and they're letting him go home. He just has to be careful. Now when can we get together?"

Chantel was glad that Harry would be all right. Her dad needed the time he shared with his friends. He didn't need more time to concentrate on her personal business or her relationship with Brogan.

"The next couple of weeks are going to be pretty hectic," she told him. "Thanksgiving is only three weeks away, and you know how insane people get near the holidays.''

''You promised to introduce Tyler to your friends.''

''And I intend to keep my promise.''

''How and when?''

Chantel resented her father's tone, almost as much as she resented his original bribe. ''I didn't make any promises about a timetable, and I didn't promise progress reports.''

Aaron was fuming. ''You're altogether too stubborn and independent, daughter,'' he snapped. ''You'd better find a good man soon, or you'll be so set in your ways that no man will have you.''

''How absolutely chauvinistic of you to issue that warning,'' Chantel replied smoothly.

''Dammit, Chantel! I'm getting old, and you're not getting any younger. You need to get serious about your life and quit playing the social butterfly.''

Her dad hadn't wasted his breath on this particular argument for quite a while. Chantel didn't have to wonder what had prompted the encore. ''Have anyone in mind?'' she asked him with a tone dripping in honey.

The question seemed to take Aaron by surprise. He hesitated and changed his tune. ''I quit giving you advice about men when you were an obstinate teenager. You never did listen, anyway.''

Chantel propped her elbows on her desk and responded softly, but firmly. ''That's right, Daddy. And I don't want you interfering in my private life any more now than I did then. You've already stretched the limits of my patience by throwing Brogan at me. I want it to stop.''

"I don't know what you mean," he insisted. He hadn't intended to throw Brogan at her. He just wanted them to get to know each other better, and they hadn't been making any effort at all.

"The deal was for you to introduce Tyler to other people," he stressed.

"I agreed to the deal on my terms," she reminded. "I want your promise to keep your nose out of anything that concerns Brogan and me."

"What concerns you will always concern me," he argued, unfazed by her flare of temper.

Chantel sighed. Why was she wasting her breath?

Aaron tried another tactic. "I felt really bad about abandoning you and Tyler Friday. Why don't you come over to dinner tonight, and I'll try to make amends."

"Sorry, Daddy, I'm booked solid all week. Why don't you offer Brogan the invitation. I'll talk to you later." She hung up the phone before he could offer any arguments.

Let him stew a while, Chantel thought. He'd find out soon enough that she and Tyler were seeing each other. If he asked her about the time they spent together, she'd swear she was just doing what he'd paid her to do.

It wasn't a very impressive start to the day, but Chantel planned to get so engrossed in her work that she wouldn't have time to worry about men and their motives.

It worked for most of the day. She saw clients, spent a considerable amount of time with investment programs, and managed to make a dent in her paperwork. It was late in the day before her personal problems invaded her professional life again.

"Do you have a minute?" Donna had knocked briefly and then entered her office.

Chantel gave her a welcoming smile. "Sure, come sit down and relax."

Donna was taller than Misty and Chantel and several years younger. She was willowy, with straight brown hair kept confined at her nape. Her youthful features held an expression of concern as she took a seat.

"I wanted to talk to you about Geoff."

Chantel grimaced inwardly, but tried not to let Donna see how distasteful she found the subject. "What about him?"

"I've always found him attractive, and I thought if the two of you were finished, that you wouldn't object to my dating him."

"He's not my favorite person, Donna, but if you're interested in him, I'm not going to harbor any resentment."

"That's what I thought. I even thought he might be interested in me once you made it clear that you didn't want him," Donna explained. Her dark eyes were clear and honest, and her quiet tone rang with sincerity.

"But when we went to the nightclub with Ken and Misty, all Geoff wanted to talk about was you. He was furious about you and Tyler Brogan. He drank more than I've ever seen him drink, and I decided he wasn't as attractive as I'd thought."

Chantel grew tense, sensing that Donna had more on her mind than girl talk. "What did he say?"

"Nothing too personal," Donna assured her. "But he kept mumbling about Cameron Industries. He said something about going back to Andersons empty-handed. Did he work for Andersons before he worked for your dad?"

"I don't think it's possible. Daddy investigates the background of his executives pretty thoroughly. He'd never hire someone who'd worked for a major competitor. He just doesn't think it's good business."

Donna nodded in agreement. "I can understand that policy, and I know Geoff wasn't fired. He quit. That's why I was surprised at how much of a grudge he seems to be harboring. He was mumbling all sorts of threats."

Chantel felt a chill race down her spine. She was convinced that Geoff Duncan could be ruthless. "What kind of threats? Against whom?"

"Nothing concrete, and he didn't mention any names. He just kept saying he'd get even, he'd show them who was the best man, and that he could get the job done."

"I don't like it." Chantel's expression was growing more grim every minute. She'd thought the bridges had been burned between Geoff and her family.

"I didn't like it much, either. I took a cab home and decided to put that man out of my mind. I figured that would be the end of it, but then he called this morning and asked me out."

"What did you say?"

Donna sometimes appeared naive, but she had a sharp mind and didn't like being used any more than Chantel. "I told him I'd check my schedule and get back with him."

"Do you still want to see him?"

"I'm convinced that he's not interested in me, but I'd like to find out how he thinks he can use me," Donna replied with a flash of spirit. "What do you think? Should I go out with him again?"

"I think it's up to you," said Chantel. "If he starts pumping you for information about me, then you'll have your answer."

"What do you think he's up to? Do you think he's jealous and wants to win you back?" Donna asked, leaning forward in her seat.

"Not likely," clipped Chantel. "He's always been more concerned about the electronics business. He used to ask me endless questions about Daddy's work."

She rocked gently in her chair as she considered Geoff's motives. She tried to remember any specific questions he'd asked. Nothing came to mind.

"Well, I think I'll call him and make a date," Donna declared as she rose from her chair. "He's piqued my curiosity now, and I'm willing to bet he's up to no good. Maybe he'll let something slip that will give us a clue."

"Or maybe he was just crying in his beer," Chantel suggested.

"I'll let you know," Donna promised as she headed for the door. "We'll teach those hotshot Romeos not to mess around with us."

Chantel laughed at her belligerent tone. Few people knew that there was a core of steel beneath Donna's youthful demeanor. Her life hadn't been an easy one, and she didn't let many people get a glimpse at the woman inside the innocent facade.

"By the way," Donna added before closing the door. "I like your Tyler Brogan. He isn't too talk-ative, but his eyes sure speak volumes, and it's all sexy. The body's not bad, either!"

Had all of her friends been aware of the attraction between her and Brogan? Chantel wondered. What had they seen in his eyes Saturday night? He hadn't acted too possessive, had he? At least, not until they'd been alone.

Was Tyler having second thoughts about becoming socialized? She hadn't heard from him since his erotic phone call after her party. Was he considering all the risks of having a romantic relationship with her? Did he think she was worth the risks?

Chantel got the answer to some of her questions later that night when Brogan telephoned. He was still willing to play her escort and help appease her father. He'd gotten the same kind of grilling from Aaron that she'd experienced. They laughed about his per-sistence, neither of them having satisfied his curiosity.

Brogan was back to his cool, calm self when he called her. Chantel was disappointed, but she resisted the urge to remind him of their other telephone con-versation. If he wanted to back off and play it cool for a while, she could do the same.

Their relationship for the rest of the week was kept under rigid control. Their conversations were impersonal. They shared dinner on Wednesday, at-tended the theater on Friday night, and spent most of Saturday at Joe and Ellen's art exhibition. Her friends were becoming accustomed to seeing them together and readily accepted Brogan.

Brogan picked her up for each event and saw her

safely to her apartment door every night. He didn't ask to come in, and she didn't invite him.

They were engaged in a private war, and each was determined to win the battle for control. Neither intended to be the one who succumbed first to temptation.

The only time Ty seemed willing to waver from his battle plan was when he kissed her goodnight. His kisses seared Chantel with a heat so intense she thought she'd melt at his feet.

She always gave as much as she received. She knew that each time he withdrew from their embrace, he was trembling as much as she was.

Saturday evening, after they left the art gallery, Brogan took Chantel to a fashionable restaurant. They just happened to run into Aaron and several of his friends. Ty was introduced to the more socially correct residents of Chicago, and he agreed to join this party of strangers without any evidence of displeasure.

Chantel grew suspicious. Had she spent last Saturday with the real Tyler Brogan, or was this pleasant, patient escort more in character? She managed to take his behavior in stride, promising herself to find out the truth once they'd reached her apartment.

Brogan walked her to her door, unlocked it with her key, and then turned watchful eyes on her. "Are you going to invite me in for a nightcap?" he queried in a totally noncommittal tone.

"Do you want a nightcap?" Chantel challenged, nearly at the end of her patience. His restraint was driving her crazy. She wanted to smack him.

"I don't want a drink, but I'd like to talk."

His eyes were hot again. Chantel felt her insides

quivering. Every time he looked at her like that, her knees grew weak. The frustrating fact was that glimpses of the fire had been too fleeting all week.

"Come on in," she told him, stepping through the door and switching on an overhead light. She tossed her coat on a nearby chair and did the same with Brogan's.

He locked the door, then moved into the living room and sat on the sofa. When Chantel entered the room, he patted the cushion beside him.

She was wearing a knee-length, black satin dress. It was simply styled, elegant, and figure hugging. The scalloped hem rose above her knees when she sat down, enhancing the long, slender length of her silk-stockinged legs.

"What did you want to talk about?" she asked coolly.

"It wasn't an accident that we ran into your dad tonight," said Brogan.

"Somehow that doesn't surprise me."

"I told him where I was taking you to eat. I also told him everywhere else we've been this week."

"That should have made him very happy," Chantel surmised, wondering where this conversation was leading.

"Would you say that you've fulfilled your obligation to your dad by accompanying me to all the right places?"

Brogan's tone was bland, almost too bland. Chantel searched his features for a clue to what he was feeling.

"I've done exactly what I promised I would do," she told him.

"You're sure?" His eyes were starting to gleam with predatory anticipation.

Chantel felt a thrill of satisfaction tingling along her nerve endings. He radiated pure male sensuality, and it did crazy things to her. "I'm absolutely positive."

Brogan had discarded his tie in the car. He slipped out of his suit jacket and tossed it aside, then shifted closer to Chantel.

"Have you honored all your other commitments for a while? No long-standing engagements or party plans for the near future?"

"Yes to the first question and no to the second," Chantel's eyes were sparkling with amusement as she answered his rapid fire questions. He was gorgeous, and he was the sexiest man she'd ever met.

"Good." There was a wealth of feeling in his one word. "Now you're not obligated to entertain me. We can forget Aaron, his business, and your friends for a while."

So that was what had kept him from making love to her all week. Chantel's smile widened. Tough guy Tyler Brogan wanted to be sure he had her absolute attention. He didn't like to share, and he didn't want her thinking about obligations when they were together.

"It's just you and me," she whispered seductively. She rose to her knees and faced him squarely. "Now do you have any other questions before I ravish you?"

Ty's breathing was already growing shallow. His body was growing hard. The sensual promise in her eyes and tone were wreaking havoc on his control. "Just one more question."

"What's that?" Chantel asked, running a finger lightly down the front of his dress shirt from the open neck to where it disappeared beneath his belt.

"Are you wearing a bra under that scrap of black fabric?"

EIGHT

Part of the bodice of Chantel's dress was made of lace over satin. The part draping her shoulders and encasing her sleeves was just lace. She never wore a bra with it.

Her shoes hit the floor as her eyes locked with Brogan's. She inched very close to him on her knees, and splayed her hands on his broad chest. "Why don't you find out for yourself?" she taunted.

In an instant she was on his lap, being dragged as close as he could hold her. His mouth came down hard on hers, displaying a need that she easily matched. For long, breathless minutes they strained to satisfy a hunger that had been gnawing all week.

Ty thrust his tongue into Chantel's mouth and challenged her tongue to a duel. She accepted the challenge, stroking and sucking his tongue until he emitted a deep, strangled moan.

His body was aching with a need so primitive he

barely understood it. He'd never wanted a woman more. He'd never spent so many long days and sleepless nights waiting until he could touch her and have her touch him.

Chantel was just as hungry for him as he was for her. She'd longed for the tenderness and passion she knew he was capable of giving her. They'd shared something incredible last week, and she wanted more, so much more.

She was holding his head tightly between her hands. Her fingers clutched at his hair while she continued to feed off his mouth. She'd been starving, and he tasted like hot spice and liquid excitement.

She tasted sweeter than anything Ty had ever known. He ground his lips against hers until they moaned in unison. She was melting in his arms, and he savored the feel of her sensuous surrender. His hands started to rove more freely over her backside.

Chantel shifted restlessly in his arms. Her breasts were full and aching. She needed closer contact. She wanted his hands and mouth on her naked flesh.

Ty found the zipper of her dress and lowered it to her waist. He eased her slightly away from him and captured her eyes while slowly lowering the bodice of her gown.

He watched her eyes dilate with excitement when the fabric slid over her thrusting nipples. She quivered when the air touched her bare flesh. His whole body began to throb with a matching agony of arousal.

"Tyler!" Chantel wanted his mouth again. She captured his lips and slid her tongue swiftly through his parted teeth. His low moan was unbearably exciting.

Ty tugged her dress over her hips and tossed it to the floor. Then he grasped Chantel by the waist and lowered her to the sofa. When she was flat on her back, he released her lips and started to explore the rest of her.

His hungry mouth and teasing tongue skipped over her cheek and down her throat. Chantel clutched at his shoulders as his hot caresses bathed her neck, then slid lower toward her breasts. Her nipples were tight and aching. She fought the urge to beg.

Tyler took his time savoring the soft mounds of her breasts. They were full and firm, her skin softer than anything he'd ever touched. When his mouth finally reached her nipples, he found them rock-hard.

The slide of his tongue over her rigid flesh made her groan in ecstasy. He used his thumb to stroke the texture of one nipple while his teeth, tongue, and lips caressed its taut twin. When she arched her back to coax for closer contact, a shudder ripped through his body.

He became more greedy and flicked his tongue from one nipple to the other. Chantel began to writhe beneath him, and every ounce of his blood seemed to be pulsing hotly, impatiently in his groin. He ground his hips against hers, but the contact only increased the ache.

Chantel's fingers clenched and unclenched in his hair. She was making wild little sounds, and he battled for control. He was feverish with desire. He tried to think through the haze of passion. He didn't want to make love to her on a sofa, fully clothed.

Dragging himself to his feet, he fought for breath, then more control. His eyes stayed glued to Chantel. She was absolutely gorgeous. Her hair was a wild tangle of curls falling over her shoulders. Her breasts were lush and rosy from his caresses. He wanted her totally naked.

Chantel's chest was heaving from the strain of trying to breathe while Brogan drove her wild with his mouth and hands. She didn't utter a tiny protest when he eased her pantyhose off her hips and rolled them down her legs.

Ty slipped his arms under her, then lifted her from the sofa and carried her to the bedroom. Chantel's arms slid around his neck in total trust. His chest constricted painfully.

When he let her down beside the bed, she reached for the buttons of his shirt and began the slow process of stripping him. Her fingers trembled on his belt buckle, but she didn't give up until she'd accomplished her objective.

When Ty felt the brush of her fingers against his zipper, he knew he didn't dare let her continue. He scooped her in his arms and lowered her to the bed, then stripped off the rest of his clothes.

Chantel's eyes went wide at the sight of his nude, highly aroused body. Her breathing became little more than a strangled panting.

"Don't panic," Ty coaxed urgently when he witnessed what he thought was feminine alarm in her eyes. He eased himself on the bed beside her. "I won't rush you," he promised gruffly, brushing a kiss over her lips. "I'll be slow and careful."

Chantel wasn't totally inexperienced, but she was

rigid with tension and frightened by her own loss of control. When Ty's mouth homed in on her breasts again, she cried out his name and began to tremble violently.

"Please, Tyler!" she moaned, clutching fistfuls of his hair.

"What, baby? Tell me what you want," he pleaded hoarsely, sliding his weight over her slender form. A flick of his fingers rid her of her silk panties, and there was nothing between their overheated bodies.

Chantel ran her hands over the smooth, hard flesh of his shoulders, her nails digging into the taut muscles. She arched her hips forcefully against the turgid evidence of his desire, and their mouths captured each other's moans.

The kiss was long and sweet and wet. Tyler was fighting desperately for control. He wanted to sheathe himself in her warmth, but he feared she couldn't accept him. He eased his body just far enough from hers to slide a hand between them and search for the heart of her desire.

His mouth trapped her cry of surprise, and then her moans of spiraling excitement. He stroked her with his finger, thumb, and palm until she was thrashing wildly beneath him.

"Tyler! Please! Please! Please!" Chantel nearly screamed as she dragged her mouth from his. He was creating an ache that was unbearable.

"Tell me what you want," he urged.

"You!" she rasped. "I want all of you!"

She had her wish in a heartbeat. Tyler swiftly joined their bodies, but he went still when she gasped raggedly.

Chantel felt him in the very depths of her body. Her muscles stretched to accommodate him, and then the hot, urgent throbbing increased to an intolerable level. Her hips involuntarily arched against his flat stomach, and she clung to his shoulders.

"Relax," Ty ground out roughly as he began to move within her. His features mirrored the strain he suffered to be gentle. He'd thought her sophisticated and experienced, but her small, tight body and her shocked reaction to his intimate caress made him doubtful.

When he felt her trying to match the rhythm of his slow movements, Ty completely lost control. He clutched her hips roughly and thrust himself into her until both of them were crying out in a release of the incredible tension.

Chantel felt tremor after tremor ripping through her body. Nothing in her experience had ever prepared her for such a violent explosion of sensation. She felt wildly elated and totally exhausted.

Ty's sweat-slick body momentarily collapsed against hers. Then he mustered the energy to take most of his weight on his forearms. His stomach stayed locked against Chantel's until he felt a renewed clenching of her feminine muscles.

He ground himself against her again until he felt the small spasms that brought her more pleasure. He would have liked to give her as much pleasure as she could stand, but he didn't have enough strength left.

They held each other tightly until their breathing had quieted somewhat. Chantel continued to stroke his head and shoulders with trembling hands.

"I never knew," she whispered softly against his ear.

Tyler found the strength to lift his head and gaze into her eyes. He was surprised but pleased when he realized what she was trying to tell him.

He'd given her a satisfaction she'd never experienced. He wished he could have gone slower and been more patient. "I'm sorry I lost control."

"Don't be sorry for anything," Chantel pleaded huskily. Her eyes were bright and adoring.

Ty smiled with masculine satisfaction. His loss of control had shocked him but not Chantel. She began to shift restlessly beneath him, and his smile widened.

"Want to make love?" he teased as he dipped his head and nibbled on her lips.

Chantel strained against him. She locked her mouth on his and kissed him long and slow, until she felt the fire begin to rekindle in his big body. Every muscle in his body flexed with renewed tension as their kiss deepened.

Ty growled low in his throat and felt her mouth curve in a smile. Sexy, sexy lady.

"Want to make love?" Chantel asked him back while bathing his ear with her tongue. She got her answer when Ty greedily sucked first one nipple and then the other. She felt the tension within her begin to rise again. She felt his body swelling within her own and knew a moment of sheer feminine delight.

"You're addictive," Ty accused gruffly. He'd never wanted a woman mere minutes after sating himself, but his body was already pulsing with new urgency.

"I like you, too," Chantel murmured as she teased the corner of his mouth with butterfly kisses. In her heart, she knew that what she was feeling for Brogan was well beyond liking. She just didn't want to worry about it now.

The second time they made love was slower, more sensual, and incredibly satisfying. They fell asleep in each other's arms.

The jarring sound of a telephone woke them both within the hour. It was going on midnight.

"Where?" mumbled Ty.

Chantel pointed to the phone on her bedside table. He grabbed the receiver and held it to her ear.

"Hello," she mumbled sleepily.

"Chantel! Are you asleep already? Where's Tyler? I thought he was with you. I can't get any answer at his apartment!" Aaron's highly agitated voice came over the lines loud enough for both of them to hear.

"Daddy, calm down. What's wrong? Why do you need Tyler?"

"Someone tried to break into my lab tonight," Aaron explained excitedly. "I need his help."

Chantel and Tyler became alert and alarmed.

"Did you call the police?"

"No," Aaron clipped. "I want Tyler to come out here, but I can't reach him."

"I'll find Tyler, Daddy," Chantel promised. The man in question was already grabbing his clothes and heading to the bathroom. "You call the police. Somebody could still be on the property. You need protection right now."

"I want Tyler!"

"I'll get Tyler!" snapped Chantel. "Now please

call the police and lock all the doors. We'll be out there as soon as possible.''

They didn't waste time. Chantel got cleaned up and ran a brush through her hair, then donned jeans and a sweater. Tyler dressed and helped her into her coat. Then they drove to the Cameron estate. The trip normally took fifteen minutes. They made it in less than ten.

Aaron was waiting for them at the front door. Chantel was glad he didn't ask how she'd managed to find Brogan so quickly.

''What happened?'' asked Tyler while shrugging out of his overcoat, then helping Chantel with hers.

''After I left the restaurant, I played some cards at George's and then came home. I went to bed, but couldn't sleep, so I decided to work in the lab a while.'' Aaron explained as he led them through the house.

''When I came out here, I found the security system destroyed. Luckily the doors won't open without the code, regardless of the condition of the system.''

The door to Aaron's lab was totally electronic. There were no doorknobs, latches, or keyholes that could be tampered with.

''So nobody actually got in?'' Ty asked.

''No, but they sure as hell did some damage. They jerked the wiring out of the box and crushed the code panel.''

''Did you call the police?'' Chantel asked impatiently.

''No, no,'' growled Aaron. ''There's not a thing they can do. Nothing was stolen.''

''The burglar had to break into the house and then destroy this system. That's a criminal action,'' Chantel argued. "Maybe he left fingerprints somewhere. How did he get into the house?"

"I don't know," replied Aaron. They all stared at the results of the vandalism. "I've checked the whole place and can't find any sign of forced entry. That's why I didn't call the police. Whoever did this must have access to the house."

Chantel's features froze into a deeper frown. "Nobody has access to this house when it's locked," she insisted. "Just you, me, and Mrs. Morley."

"That's what I thought," said Aaron. "But obviously we're both wrong."

"Where is Mrs. Morley?" asked Ty.

"She spends her weekends in town with a sister."

"How many people know she's gone on weekends?"

"Probably everybody who knows us," said Chantel.

"So anyone who knew Aaron was going to town for dinner also knew that the house would be empty?"

"I guess so," said Aaron, working with the wiring that had been torn from the wall. "But nobody can get past the outside security without a key and the code."

Ty was shaking his head. "But somebody who's familiar with the system, maybe a frequent guest, would know what was needed?"

Chantel didn't like the direction of his thoughts. "You think that a friend of the family did this?"

"Not necessarily a friend, but someone who's had access in the past."

"Nobody has ever been given a key and the code."

"Someone could have stolen a key, had a copy made, and watched you or your dad punch in a code.

If they were considering a burglary, they'd have been more observant than the casual guest.''

Tyler's theory made sense, but Chantel didn't like it one bit. That would mean that she or her dad had brought someone into the house who'd come with the intention of invading their privacy.

"You checked all the windows, doors, vents, any opening that could be used?" Ty asked Aaron.

"We need to check again. The house is big, and I was in a hurry," Aaron replied. "But I didn't find any obvious signs of a break-in."

"I still think you should call the police!" Chantel insisted. "They have people who are trained for this kind of investigation."

Both men ignored her and continued to search the immediate area for clues. The intruder had been neat except for the damage to the security system. Chantel knew they weren't going to call for help. Tyler and her father were very much alike when it came to stubbornness.

"Are you sure there wasn't any damage or theft in the lab?" she asked Aaron.

"I can't be sure until I can get in there. I can't get in there until I rebuild this security system and use the proper code."

"There's no other entrance to the lab?" asked Ty.

"Not even a window," Aaron explained. "This is the only door, and the only outside vent is protected by steel fencing encased in concrete."

Ty allowed himself a grin. When Aaron secured a building, he thought of everything. Too bad he hadn't seen the need to secure his home as well as his lab.

"I guess all we can do is check the house again," said Ty.

"And have all new locks and codes installed to-morrow," put in Chantel.

"Why don't you work on the security system, Aaron, and Chantel can show me the rest of the house," Ty suggested. "We'll check for anything out of the ordinary."

When Chantel suggested they split up, Ty quickly vetoed the idea. "I don't know the house, and we can't be sure the intruder is gone."

Chantel didn't like that idea, either.

"I'll get some tools and get to work here," said Aaron. "It shouldn't take too long to rewire the system."

Tyler and Chantel did a slow and thorough check of every room on the bottom level of the house and headed upstairs. They went to the attic first, then back to the second story. There were seven bedrooms and three bathrooms. They went through each of them carefully but found nothing out of place.

The last room they investigated was Chantel's room. Most of her belongings had been moved to her apartment, but she used her old room occasionally and kept some personal items there. Ty made sure all the windows were secure, and then he began to explore.

Pink and lavender were the prominent colors of the decor, with light wood and wicker furnishings. It was a very feminine room that held memorabilia from the many stages of Chantel's life. There was everything from toys to investment journals. Tyler was intrigued.

"Do you mind?" he asked, picking up a stuffed doll from a cabinet filled with every size and shape of stuffed animal.

Chantel shook her head negatively, then went to stand near him. "Her name is Maria," she explained. "I've had her since I was ten."

"She looks well-loved."

"She looks worn out," countered Chantel, taking the ragged doll from his hand. Maria had heard many sob stories and girlish secrets over the years.

"Isn't that the same thing when you describe dolls?"

"I guess."

"What about all the rest of them?"

"Collected over the years. I probably should give them away, but I've just never gotten around to it."

"And the books?" Ty asked, nodding toward a bookcase that covered one wall.

The books were a collection of everything from Dr. Seuss to college level algebra. "I have a hard time parting with books," Chantel explained with a grin.

Tyler returned her grin. He understood. He and his dad had become adept at building shelves. His room at home held several hundred books. He always planned to sort them and get rid of a few, but he never did.

"We both love books," Ty told her, drawing her into his arms. "I guess we have something in common, Ms. Cameron."

"Amazing," she teased, wrapping her arms around his waist. When she lifted her face for a kiss, he swiftly brought his mouth down on hers, locking their lips.

Their tongues tangled, and they strained a little closer to each other. The kiss was long and sweet and satisfying. When it was necessary to catch their breath, Ty cradled her face in one palm and gently stroked her cheek with his thumb. His eyes were turbulent with emotion when they locked with Chantel's.

"I didn't get a chance to say thank you," he told her gruffly.

He was saying thank you for the incredible loving they'd shared. Chantel felt the warmth of a blush creeping over her cheeks. She wasn't sure how to respond.

"Should I say you're very welcome?" she asked him shyly. Ty's answering smile made her heart skip a beat. He was absolutely gorgeous when he smiled. His eyes were as dark as molasses, and their message was distinctly intimate.

Ty loved the pink of her cheeks and the warmth he felt beneath his fingers. She was such an intriguing mixture of sophistication and innocence.

"I got the impression that you don't trust too many men with the gift you gave me."

Chantel lowered her lashes and felt the heat in her cheeks increase. She'd hoped he wouldn't notice how inexperienced she was when it came to making love. Apparently he had enough experience to recognize a novice.

"Chantel," he murmured softly, brushing a kiss across her lips. "I wasn't criticizing. You're the sexiest, most passionate woman I've ever known. Nothing in my experience has ever been as perfect as making love to you.''

Her lungs constricted, and her heart thudded heavily. She resorted to flippancy to cover her turbulent reaction to his words. "I'll bet you say that to all the girls!"

"Never!" Ty's tone was low and fierce. "There haven't been that many women. I'm selective, and you're too special for words."

Elation coursed through Chantel. She felt the same way about him. Ty was more special than he knew. He made her proud of her femininity. He made her feel desirable. He'd unleashed a passionate nature that she'd never really explored.

She tightened her hold on him and stood on tiptoe to offer him her mouth. Ty's arms tightened around her, lifting her closer. Their mouths met in an explosion of emotion. Neither of them seemed able to get their fill of the other.

Aaron's voice finally penetrated the haze of shared bliss. Tyler managed to drag his lips from Chantel's. He was breathing heavily. His whole body was heavy with need again. He could hardly believe the effect Chantel had on his control.

"Your dad's calling us," he declared hoarsely.

Chantel just groaned. She didn't want to talk to anyone else. She just wanted to be alone with Tyler.

"Coming!" Ty shouted in response to Aaron's next call. He reluctantly eased his hold on Chantel.

"I guess we'd better go see if Daddy has the security system fixed," she said.

"I guess," agreed Tyler, his tone and smile telling her that he wasn't happy at the interruption either.

Aaron had managed to do enough rewiring to gain access to his lab. They found him searching for any sign of vandalism, and they told him they hadn't found anything unusual in the rest of the house.

"Nothing's been touched in here," he declared in satisfaction. "I'll bet our would-be thief is feeling pretty frustrated."

Tyler and Chantel frowned. They didn't like to think about what a frustrated thief might try next.

"Do you think he planned to steal your robot?" Chantel asked her dad.

"I doubt it," replied Aaron. "It wouldn't do anyone much good without the data. My guess is that someone hopes to steal my research files and build their own robot."

"Who knows how far your experiments have advanced?" asked Tyler. "Do you know anyone who's working on a similar project and might be willing to pay well for the data?"

"Not right offhand," said Aaron. "But I plan to give it a lot of thought. I'll start asking questions and do some investigating. We might as well lock up here and get some sleep. It's getting late. You two can spend the night. There's plenty of room."

Chantel flashed Ty a look that assured him she'd rather spend the night with him. Still, neither of them wanted Aaron to be left alone. They'd have to sleep in separate rooms tonight.

Tyler's expression told her he shared her feelings. Then he turned his attention to Aaron. "You'd better hire a security guard until we find out who's behind this break-in."

"I'll see about it first thing Monday," Aaron agreed.

Chantel couldn't believe her ears. If she'd have suggested any kind of guard for her father, he'd have flatly refused to consider the idea. Apparently Tyler's concern held more weight, or else Aaron was more worried than he wanted her to know.

NINE

Though the next day was Sunday, Aaron managed to get a security team to the house and have all his locks changed.

When Tyler and Chantel were satisfied that the house was secure, they went home to their respective apartments, showered, changed clothes, and headed for the teen center where they'd planned to help with some painting.

The shelter for pregnant teenagers was a huge old brownstone building in a poor but respectable neighborhood. Chantel had always felt completely at home in the shelter. She'd been visiting on a regular basis for as long as she could remember.

"This place is nearly as big as your dad's house," commented Tyler as he helped her from the car.

"My mother told me it was originally the showplace home of one of Chicago's infamous gangsters. She said it used to have crystal chandeliers and solid gold fixtures in every room, but those were sold a long time ago for taxes and upkeep. This center was her pet project.''

"How many rooms?'' asked Ty. He let his eyes roam over the aging but still impressive architecture.

"Twenty,'' Chantel replied as she stepped on the porch and rang the doorbell. "But that doesn't include the three sections of the basement or the top story. With enough money, the attic could be converted into a couple more bedrooms.''

"Won't your dad's contributions help?''

"Eventually,'' Chantel agreed. "But the money has to be carefully budgeted for a few years until the investments begin to show profit and the center's financial future can be secured. Government funding is unreliable at best.''

"You handle all the investments?'' asked Tyler. He'd learned a little about her work this past week.

"Yes. For the most part, the money will be invested in blue chip securities. A very small percentage will go for high-risk, high-yield stocks.''

"Sounds sensible.''

"I'm a sensible investment agent.''

Ty gave her a grin. Chantel loved his grin.

The front door opened, and they were greeted by a very pregnant young girl wearing a paint-splattered smock. She was short, with dark hair and dark, guarded eyes.

"I thought I heard the doorbell. I wasn't sure.''

That was understandable. The music blaring from the interior of the house was deafening.

"No problem,'' said Chantel with a grin. She and

Tyler entered the house as their hostess screamed for someone to turn down the radio.

When it was quieter, Chantel smiled at the teen. "How are you feeling, Patty? Looks like you've been painting already."

The teenager gave Chantel a smile. "I've just been getting everything ready. This is my painting shirt; that's why it's so colorful."

Chantel laughed as she and Tyler hung their coats over a hall rack. Her jeans and sweatshirt also had some permanent paint stains.

"Patty, this is Tyler Brogan, a friend of mine who's volunteered to help today."

The young girl glanced at Tyler, but the smile slipped from her face, and she didn't offer a hand or word in greeting. "We can use somebody for the high places," was her only comment as she turned to leave them.

Tyler shot Chantel a questioning glance.

"I'm going to show Tyler around. Is Annette here?" Chantel asked Patty's retreating form.

"She's still at church, some kind of special dinner they're having," Patty offered. "She won't be back until this evening." Then she was gone.

"Annette Danfield is the housemother, midwife, psychologist, and all-round caretaker of this place," Chantel explained. "I'm sorry you won't get to meet her."

"Does she give visitors as cool a greeting a Miss Patty?" Ty felt compelled to ask.

Chantel grinned. "Most of the girls here aren't too fond of men during their stay. Annette's a sweetheart. She likes everybody."

"There isn't anyone here right now who's afraid of men, is there?" asked Ty, after comprehending the reason for his cool reception.

Chantel was touched by his concern for the emotional fragility of the pregnant teens. "There are ten pregnant teens in residence right now. Only one of them is a rape victim, but she's not afraid of men in general. The majority of the girls become more anti-male as their pregnancies progress."

"And Patty is pretty far along?"

"She's due at the end of the month."

"I'll try to steer clear of her."

Chantel laughed and slipped an arm in his, leading him through the foyer to show him the adjoining rooms. "Patty's the interior decorator on this project, so she'll be your boss for most of the day."

"Is it safe for her to be painting?"

Chantel felt another thrill at his sensitivity and concern. "We use nontoxic paint and make sure the rooms are well-ventilated. I try to see that she doesn't work too long without a break or do anything too strenuous, but she's full of energy. Annette says she won't hurt herself or the baby."

Tyler wasn't pacified. His continued frown made Chantel laugh. "Healthy pregnant women can function normally, Brogan. They aren't invalids," she teased.

"She's just a baby, herself," he growled. "Where's her family? Where's the guy who got her pregnant?"

Chantel's amusement ended on a heavy sigh. She'd asked the same questions many times over the years. "Some of these girls have been kicked out of their homes and abandoned by their boyfriends. Some are too independent to accept help from their families. Others are runaways who refuse to contact their parents. Some don't know who the father of the child is. Many of them give the babies up for adoption.''

''Quite a variety,'' he said as he surveyed the first of many rooms in the house. ''There's no particular criteria for letting them stay here?''

''Only that they help with the chores and practice healthy lifestyles while they're here. They have to eat right, take their vitamins, and have regular checkups.''

Tyler continued to ask questions as Chantel showed him through the downstairs rooms. The house had a huge kitchen and an even bigger dining room. There was a central living room, a game room, and several smaller sitting rooms. Chantel introduced Tyler to the many occupants as they were encountered.

The radio was turned on again, but at a lower volume. ''If you visit here,'' Chantel explained, ''you have to get used to the music or wear earplugs. I think the radios play twenty-four hours a day.''

''That doesn't surprise me,'' he told her. ''One of my mom's most-repeated phrases was 'turn down the radio.' ''

Chantel had been surprised to learn that he came from a fairly large family. He had two brothers and a sister, yet he seemed like such a loner.

''I think my mother might have said that a few times, too,'' she confessed. ''For a while I was into heavy metal.''

Tyler groaned.

"Never appealed to you?" she quipped.

"Never."

Chantel laughed and directed him to the room where they were going to be painting. It was the library, but it had been neglected over the years when the short supply of funds had been used strictly for necessities.

"This is the last room downstairs to be remodeled," she told him. "Patty, Annette, and various other helpers have slowly given the other ground-level rooms a face-lift, but there's still a lot of work to be done upstairs. We're trying to do each room as the occupants leave."

"Quite an undertaking," said Tyler as he glanced around the room.

"You'd better believe it."

"A contractor would have cost too much?"

"Way too much," Chantel replied.

"If this was your mother's project, why hasn't your dad helped with the funding before this?"

Chantel had often voiced the same question. "She claimed it was her independent spirit. She'd work her tail off to raise funds and help with the upkeep, but she refused to ask Daddy for money."

"You didn't mind asking him."

"Not in the least," chimed Chantel. "I have no reservations about taking his money. He'll just use it as a tax write-off anyway."

Tyler gave her a grin that made her heart do a little flip-flop. He looked so stern and serious until he smiled. Then the warmth in his eyes was breathtaking.

"Where do we start?" Ty asked, dragging his eyes from Chantel. He'd been aching to hold her all morning. If he wasn't careful, he'd make a fool of himself by dragging her into his arms and shocking a house full of impressionable young girls.

"Patty?" Chantel turned to their resident decorator. She hoped the teenager didn't understand the cause of her heightened color. Just looking at Tyler excited her.

Patty pulled the headphones from her ears and explained the plans to Chantel. "We decided to do this room in pale gold. We've got the paint, and varnish for the shelves, but I want to do the shelves last because I'll have to leave."

"The varnish is dangerous?" asked Tyler.

"It's not toxic, but Annette said the oil base products have too strong an odor. She says it'll make me sick."

"It makes me sick, and I'm not pregnant," said Chantel as she stirred the paint.

"I'll do the shelves last," Tyler agreed. Then he grabbed a stepladder and moved it to one of the three walls that needed painting. "I'll do the high part."

Chantel handed him a bucket of paint and a large brush. She was pleased by his willingness to help. The one time she'd brought Geoff to the center, he'd acted like he was afraid he might get dirty.

"Patty and I will paint around the baseboard and as high as we can reach."

"Don't strain yourselves," Tyler warned fiercely.

Patty and Chantel exchanged a grin, and the younger girl rolled her eyes. He'd directed his comment to both of them, but it was obvious he didn't want Patty to do anything that might hurt her.

"Men!" Patty mouthed to Chantel, pretending his concern was silly. The flush on her cheeks and light in her eyes told a different story. Tyler had won acceptance with no more than his usual, succinct style of communicating.

The three of them worked for the next hour with a minimum of conversation. Chantel noticed that Patty put her earphones aside and was more verbal than usual, especially in the presence of a man. She wondered if Tyler had ever considered psychology as a profession.

Other members of the household, in various stages of pregnancy, stopped by the room to see the progress, but they didn't stay long or offer to help. Chantel was sure they were more interested in Tyler than painting.

It was well after noon before Patty laid down her brush. "I'm starving. You guys want some lunch?"

Chantel looked at Tyler, temporarily distracted by the way his worn jeans hugged his long legs and slim hips. Blushing at her own thoughts, she asked, "Are you hungry?"

"Not right now."

"We didn't eat breakfast until almost eleven," Chantel told Patty. "Go ahead and eat without us."

"Okay," said Patty, stifling a yawn.

Chantel grinned. "You're welcome to take a nap after you eat, too. It won't take long for Tyler and me to finish the walls. Then you'll have to be out of here anyway while he varnishes."

"You're sure you don't mind?"

"Positive."

Patty glanced at Tyler and back to Chantel. "I might take a little nap after lunch," she said. "I get sleepier now that the baby's getting so big."

"We'll call you before we leave," promised Chantel.

Patty gave her a smile and left the room.

"She's carrying a lot of extra weight, isn't she?" asked Tyler.

"She's nearly full-term. I imagine she's starting to feel a lot more strain now."

"How old is she?"

"She's one of the youngest, only fourteen."

Tyler mumbled a string of curses, slapping on the paint with unnecessary force. "Why is she here?"

"I don't ask for particulars anymore," Chantel explained. "Patty isn't one to share confidences."

"What will she do with the baby?"

"She's giving it up for adoption. She's already met the adoptive parents. They want to be with her during her labor and delivery, and she's satisfied that she's doing what's best for the baby."

Tyler grunted, then was quiet for a while. When he stopped painting so furiously, Chantel approached the stepladder and laid a hand on his thigh. She felt his muscle quiver and grinned up at him.

"You must like living dangerously," he growled, glancing at the slim fingers resting on his leg and then at the brush in his hand. "Grabbing a man's thigh could cause an accident and result in serious injury."

"Really?" she teased, running her fingers over the smooth denim of his jeans. "Is your thigh sensitive?"

Tyler groaned, and she felt the muscles beneath her fingers flexing again.

"Did you want something?"

"The only spot left to paint is behind you," Chantel explained, removing her hand. Tyler had almost finished the upper half of the room, alternately using a brush and roller. Patty and Chantel had done most of the bottom half, but the only section left was behind the stepladder.

"I'm almost done," he told her, making one final sweep over the wall.

When he stepped down and was standing in front of Chantel, he touched her nose with the tip of the paintbrush. "You have paint on your nose."

"Tyler! That was mean!" she exclaimed, rubbing her nose with the sleeve of her shirt.

"Not as mean as playing with a guy's thigh when you know he can't reciprocate."

Chantel burst out laughing. He was outrageous, and she loved it. "All right. We're even. Now let's cooperate and finish this wall."

"Deal," he agreed, his grin wicked.

A little later, Ty commented on the nature of the center. "I guess it's easy to get hooked on helping here, isn't it?"

"Not for everyone," Chantel replied. "My mother spent so much time here that I got a little jealous when I was younger."

"You obviously got over it."

"Yes." Chantel's response was brief as she mulled over the possibility of telling him the whole truth.

She wondered how he would take the news. If he had some kind of hang-up about illegitimate children, she needed to know before she fell any deeper in love with him.

"I used to wonder why my mother was so devoted to this place," Chantel began a bit nervously.

Tyler thought he knew why. Aaron had explained his wife's unwed state when Chantel was born. He imagined she'd found support at this center, but he didn't think Chantel knew that. She stunned him with her next statement.

"I was born here."

Tyler stopped painting and stared at her. "In this house?"

"Yes," continued Chantel, concentrating on the wall she was painting. She'd come to terms with the nature of her birth, but she'd never tried to explain to anyone.

"When my mother was dying, she kept asking me to promise I would take care of Daddy. It seemed the most important thing to her right then. I kept promising, and she kept fretting about protecting him. Sometimes she was barely conscious, and she'd mumble things I didn't understand. I caught an occasional phrase and one specific word: adopted."

Chantel was finding it harder than she thought to talk about her mother's death and her subsequent findings. "Tyler, will you promise me you'll never tell a soul what I'm about to tell you?"

Tyler looked at her earnest expression and hesitated. He was wary of any more promises. Chantel's secret might be more than he wanted to handle.

"Tyler?" she prodded.

"I promise."

Chantel sighed and began to paint again. "My dad and I both gave blood when Mother was ill. She had type "O" blood which is a universal donor and mixes with any type. I found out Daddy has an unusual blood type, and that my blood couldn't possibly be a blend of the two."

"How did your dad explain that?"

"He didn't. I just happened to see the paperwork and asked the medical staff some questions. I don't suppose he gave it a thought at the time. He was beside himself with worry about mother."

"And you never mentioned it to him?"

"No, but after Mother died I came to Annette. I knew she'd been here for more than thirty years."

"She filled in the details?"

"My mother had instructed her to tell me the whole truth if I ever asked. Annette said my mother had come to her as an eighteen-year-old college freshman in love with one of her professors.

"When she told him she was pregnant, she found out he had a wife, and later that she was just one of a long list of his 'conquests.' He didn't want anything to do with her after that."

Tyler was swearing again, and Chantel was encouraged to tell him more. "My mother's parents lived out of state, and she didn't want to go home to them in disgrace."

"So she came here."

"Yes. She quit school, got a job, and came to Annette. She lived here until I was born. She met

Daddy a couple months later, they were married, and he legally adopted me.''

Chantel had been painting the same spot for more than ten minutes. Tyler took the brush from her hand and turned her into his arms. She tilted her head up to look at him.

''Why haven't you ever discussed this with your dad?'' he asked softly.

''When I first found out, we were both too busy trying to comfort each other over the loss of Mother. I didn't have the heart. Later I decided that it was his secret, and I'd have to wait until he was ready to share it.''

''Weren't you bitter and angry with both of them?'' Tyler asked. He still got angry when he thought of how his mom had kept the truth from him.

''At first I was bitter because I thought they'd treated me like a child. I thought they didn't respect me as an intelligent adult. It still hurts to think they might have worried about how I would react,'' said Chantel, shifting closer to the heat of his body.

Tyler held her closer. ''Weren't you curious about your biological father?''

''Not a lot. I knew he was despicable.''

''You don't have any interest in finding him?''

''Annette said he was killed in a car wreck. His wife had divorced him, and he didn't have any children. There was no reason to delve into his background.''

''And no reason to broach the subject with your dad?''

Chantel stood on her tiptoes and brushed a kiss

over his lips. He'd never know how much it meant to have him listen without being judgmental.

"I've forgiven Daddy," she declared. "I think I'll understand if he never tells me the whole truth."

Tyler didn't have such a forgiving nature. "How can you forgive him and not resent his silence?"

"First, because he's been the most loving and supporting father anyone could want," Chantel explained, smoothing her hands over the soft fabric of his shirt.

"And secondly, because I considered the fact that he was raised in a generation of people who believed you had to protect your loved ones from any kind of unpleasantness. In my father's time, the words *sex* and *pregnancy* weren't even said out loud. Unwed mothers were only discussed in whispers and never with the children. It's just his way."

Tyler gave serious thought to her words. It had been his mother's way, too. He'd often protested that she was overprotective. Maybe she'd been ashamed to share the truth with him. Maybe protecting him had been more important.

For the first time since learning that Aaron was his father, Tyler viewed the situation from a different angle. Maybe he'd judged his mother too harshly. The beautiful woman in his arms had a much deeper insight into human nature.

"You're incredibly special. Do you know that?" he asked Chantel, his eyes searing her with heated intensity.

She fought for breath. His words, and the look in his eyes, created a quivering response throughout her body. She didn't have to worry about him thinking less of her.

"You're the one who's special," she insisted throatily, sliding her arms around his neck.

Tyler held her close and sought her mouth with his. Lips and teeth parted as tongues sought their mates. He feasted hungrily on the addictive taste of her. They kissed until neither of them had a breath left in their bodies. Then they kissed again, and again, and strained closer.

TEN

Tyler paced his office on Monday morning, irritated by his lack of enthusiasm for the work that needed to be done. He didn't want to study contract terms. He wanted Chantel. He wanted to hold her. Kiss her. Love her.

It had nearly killed him to take her home and leave her last night without making love to her. He knew she'd expected it, but he'd been determined to control his growing obsession with her. His determination had won him a long, lonely night of frustration.

He'd never needed and wanted a woman like he did Chantel. The only time he'd come close was with Susan. She'd told him he smothered her, that he was oversexed and too possessive. Then she'd seduced his brother.

Ty refused to make the same mistakes with Chantel. He cared too much, even though he knew it was a mistake. Falling for her was like lighting a fuse to a keg of dynamite. As long as the secret of his real identity was between them, they had no future.

He couldn't stop thinking about Chantel's secret. He'd promised not to tell anyone. He'd promised not to tell anyone Aaron's secret. The two people who were beginning to mean so much to him both had the same secret, yet nobody wanted to share it.

The ringing of the phone gave him something to do with his frustrated energy. "Brogan."

"Ty? It's Marie. Have I called at a bad time?"

Tyler relaxed at the sound of his sister's voice. He dropped into his chair. "No, not at all. I can't seem to concentrate on anything this morning."

"You must be sick!" she teased. "You're the most focused person I know."

Tyler's lips curved in a smile. "Did you want something in particular, or did you just call to harass me?"

Marie laughed. "Actually, I called to invite you to dinner."

"California is a little far to come for a meal," he responded lightly. "Even if it's home-cooked."

"This is a big one."

He tried to remember if it was anybody's birthday, or if there was any other special occasion he'd forgotten.

"The major family meal of the year," she prompted.

"I'll need a bigger clue than that," Ty admitted.

Marie sighed heavily. "How about Indians, pilgrims, and turkeys."

Tyler chuckled. "It's not Christmas, yet, is it?" he continued to tease. "My calendar says November."

"Thanksgiving, big brother, Thanksgiving," Marie stated with mock-severity. "How can you forget Thanksgiving?"

"I've had other things on my mind."

"Don't you always?"

"A mind is a terrible thing to waste," he argued.

"Okay, okay, I give up," said Marie. "Thanksgiving is coming, and I wondered if you'd come home. It would be nice to have a family dinner. I know Christmas will be too hectic for everyone, so this might be our only chance."

Tyler glanced at the gray, rainy weather outside his window and knew it would be great to spend some time in southern California. Besides, his relationship with Chantel was getting serious. He'd better introduce her to his brothers before he got any more involved.

"Am I allowed to bring a guest?" he asked.

There was a brief hesitation on the other end of the line. "Male or female?" asked Marie.

"Most definitely female," said Ty.

He knew Marie wouldn't like it. She was hoping he'd hate Chicago and move home. She had hoped that nothing and no one in Chicago would appeal to him.

"How serious is it?"

"How serious is what?"

"This woman. You can't have known her more than a couple months. Who is she? How serious are you about her?"

"None of your business, little sister. If she's not welcome, I won't come. It's that simple."

"Will you be sharing a bedroom?"

"No," Ty growled in a warning tone.

"The guest room is a mess, but she could use Mom and Dad's room. We had it remodeled, it just needs a little cleaning, and she'd have her own bath. Is she a big eater? I want to be sure and have enough food."

"Don't worry about it. I'm not even sure she can come. She usually has a pretty full calendar."

Marie groaned. "Not another social butterfly, Tyler! You have a knack for dating the wrong type of woman. I hope she's brother-proof."

His sister was totally lacking in tact. She always said the first thing that popped into her mind. "If the lady prefers Shawn or Peter to me, then she's not worth worrying about, is she?"

"I suppose not, but I don't want the weekend ruined by all that macho male competitiveness and antagonism. I want this to be a pleasant, happy holiday."

"I'll be on my best behavior."

"I know. I know all about your behavior," fretted Marie. "I've watched this game enough. Shawn and Peter start preening and competing. You withdraw altogether. I hate it."

"Would you rather I didn't come?"

Marie sighed. "I want you to come."

"I'll check with Chantel and get back with you."

"Chantel?"

"That's the lady's name."

"It sounds kind of high-class. Is she one of those

elegant society queens who never gets her hands dirty?''

Tyler had an image of Chantel with paint on her nose. ''We spent yesterday painting someone's library, and Chantel had more paint on her than the walls did.''

Marie was somewhat mollified and said goodbye after a few more minutes of conversation. Ty hung up the phone, then lifted the receiver again to call Chantel's private line at her office.

''Hello?''

The sound of her voice sent a ripple of pleasure through him. ''Is this the best investment agent in Chicago?'' he asked.

He heard the smile in her voice when she replied. ''Good morning, Tyler. Did you want some investment advice?''

''Not really,'' he retorted laconically, then smiled at the sound of her husky laughter. ''Are you busy?''

''I should be,'' said Chantel, ''but I can't seem to get motivated this morning.''

He knew the feeling. Maybe he should have spent last night making love to her. Then they'd have an excuse for today's restlessness. Or maybe they wouldn't be restless.

''Tyler?''

''Sorry. I got distracted for a minute,'' he told her, feeling warmth steal up his neck. All his blood had rushed to his groin at the thought of making love to her.

''What distracted you?''

''It was something very intimate. You'd be shocked.''

"Try me."

"Not over the phone, but I'll explain some time when we're alone."

"Mmm, that interesting, huh?" she taunted. "Did you call just to tell me you couldn't tell me what you've been thinking?"

"No, I called to invite you to Thanksgiving dinner. Do you already have plans?"

"Not yet."

"What about your dad?"

"He always goes hunting for the whole weekend. It's his annual back-to-nature outing with the guys."

"Then how about flying to California with me?"

Chantel caught her breath and wondered if he was teasing. "Why California?"

"My sister just called and asked me to come home for Thanksgiving weekend. I told her I'd come if you wanted to come with me."

"Honestly?"

"Honestly. How about it?"

Chantel glanced at the dark skies outside her window. Sunny California sounded wildly appealing. A weekend with Tyler sounded even better. "You're sure your family won't mind having me?"

"I'm sure."

"Tyler!" she exclaimed, laughing. "You really need to learn to speak in longer, more complete sentences."

"Why?"

Chantel laughed harder. "You're hopeless!"

Tyler's tone was thick with amusement when he responded. "Does that mean you accept the invitation? Think of all the time you'll have to reform me.''

"I accept," she declared. "But I'm not going to waste time beating my head against a brick wall. I'll settle for some good food, good company, and sunshine."

"We should be able to provide the basics. I'll make flight reservations for Wednesday evening."

"I can make my own reservations."

"My treat. You're my guest, so don't argue."

Chantel was so happy with the invitation, that she didn't argue. "I wouldn't dream of it."

"Will I see you tonight?"

"Do you want to?"

"Yes."

"Please don't elaborate," she teased.

"Any elaboration would be x-rated," Ty confessed.

Warmth poured through Chantel. Tonight seemed so far away. "I'll cook dinner if you don't mind eating at my place."

"What time?" Ty's voice was low and gruff. He couldn't hide his desire to see her.

"Whenever you like," said Chantel. "I'll probably be home by six."

"I'll see you then."

Chantel hung up the phone. Her eyes were shining, and she was wearing a dreamy smile. She'd forgotten that Donna and Misty were both in her office until Donna spoke.

"I take it that was Tyler Brogan."

"And that he's issued an immoral invitation," Misty supplied.

Chantel swung around in her chair and faced the

other two, trying to regain her composure. "Actually, it wasn't immoral. He invited me to spend Thanksgiving with him and his family. It's a very old-fashioned, traditional invitation."

"So what about making reservations?" asked Misty.

"Well," Chantel hedged. "his home happens to be in California."

She laughed as her friends screeched in amazement.

"You're breaking another rule for that man!" cried Misty. "You said you'd never go away with someone who wasn't talking permanent commitment."

"It's not like we're going to a lover's retreat," Chantel argued. "We'll be spending the weekend with his family." At least, she supposed they would.

"He's moving a little fast, isn't he?" worried Donna.

Chantel couldn't deny that. On the one hand, he was moving very fast. On the other hand, the physical one, he'd been as slow as molasses. She'd been stunned when he'd left her last night. She'd badly wanted him to stay.

Had he meant it when he'd called her special, or had he been trying to spare her feelings? Had he found her inexperience disappointing? Did he still want her or was all his sexy talk just for show? Did she lack whatever it took to keep a man interested?

"Earth to Chantel," chimed Misty.

"I'm sorry," she told her friends. "What was the last question?"

"We're wasting our breath," said Donna.

"Is there anything else you wanted to get typed today?" asked Misty. "I'd better get back to work."

"I'll need a copy of the investment agenda I drew up for Mr. Forsythe. That's all I need this morning."

"I'll take care of it right now," said Misty as she headed for her own office.

"How about you, Donna? Anything else?"

"Not work related," Donna responded as she rose from her chair. "I was just going to mention that I made a date with Geoff for last Saturday, but he stood me up."

"Stood you up?"

"Yeah, he called me a few minutes before he was supposed to pick me up and canceled our date. He said he had an emergency and promised to make it up to me."

"He didn't explain his emergency?"

"Not a word. Just a last-minute brush-off."

"That's strange," said Chantel.

"The man is strange," Donna declared. "I think he's strung out for some reason, or in some kind of trouble. He sounded nervous and impatient."

"Maybe it really was an emergency situation."

Donna shrugged. "I was all dressed up with no where to go, then I remembered the country club out by your dad's house. They have a singles' party every Saturday night and you don't have to be a member."

"Did you go to the club?" Chantel asked, remembering her own hurried trip in that direction Saturday night.

"Yeah, and I could have sworn I passed Geoff heading back to town on the same road."

Chantel's eyes widened. "On the road that goes past Daddy's house?"

"Uh huh."

"Right after he called you?"

"An hour or so later."

He would have had time to break his date with Donna, drive to her dad's, break into the house, and then head back to town. Geoff had been to the house many times, and it was possible he had a key. He'd often started her car to get it warm and used her keys to open her apartment door. Once he'd even taken them home by mistake.

Had it been a mistake? Or had he been planning to break into her dad's house all along? He'd watched her punch in the code several times, and he'd always been quick with numbers.

"Chantel?"

"I'm sorry, Donna. My mind keeps drifting. Thanks for the information about Geoff. It might be important."

"No problem. I hope he isn't going to cause you or your dad any trouble."

Chantel sighed. "I hope not, too."

"I'd better get to work. I'll let you know if I hear from Geoff again."

"Thanks," said Chantel, her head spinning with unpleasant thoughts. She watched Donna leave her office. What was Geoff up to? Had he used her all along to gain access to her dad's research data? Had he really wanted to be CEO of Cameron Industries, or had that just been a cover for a more devious quest?

She'd have to tell Tyler what she suspected and see if he could make sense of it. She'd tell him tonight. She was seeing Tyler tonight. The thought brought a smile back to her lips.

Chantel's doorbell rang at 6:30 that evening. She'd slipped away from work early, started dinner, and taken a quick shower. Her business suit had been replaced by a lavender silk jumpsuit. The fabric swished as she walked quickly to the door.

Tyler smiled when he saw her, and Chantel's pulse accelerated at the sight of him. He was wearing jeans and an off-white, cable-knit sweater that emphasized his broad shoulders. His thick hair looked a little mussed, and his eyes looked hungry.

"Hi, come on in. Where's your coat?" Chantel sounded a little breathless as she invited him in and closed the door.

"It's not that cold, and I didn't want to mess with it," Tyler explained, and then handed her one perfect red rose, surrounded by baby's breath, and wrapped in tissue paper. "For the hostess," he said lightly.

Chantel brought the rose to her face and inhaled the delicate aroma. "Thank you." She couldn't remember ever being so touched by such a simple gift.

"The florist said red roses are for passion, so I wanted to buy a couple dozen. But she talked me into buying just one. What do you think?" he teased lightly.

"Smart lady," Chantel told him. Men had tried to impress her with roses by the dozen. One special man brought her one rose. "She probably doesn't own the business, but she's definitely an asset."

"She suggested that 'my lady' would probably be pleased enough to give me a kiss." His eyes were alight with sensual challenge. Tyler in a teasing mood was irresistible.

"Really?" Chantel drawled, pretending to give the idea careful consideration.

"Really."

"Did she say it should be a nice little kiss of gratitude, or a long, deep, passionate kiss in respect for the rose?"

Tyler was already gathering her in his arms and pulling her close to him. His eyes had darkened at her description of the kiss he wanted.

Chantel's arms went around his shoulders, one hand pressing his gift against his back. Their eyes locked, and she knew the word games were over. Tyler had the look of a man who'd lost patience with words. She was sure she had an identical expression on her face.

The first brush of his mouth made her lips tremble. He was so gentle, so sensitive to her need for tenderness. He didn't rush, but coaxed her lips apart as if they were sharing their first, tentative kiss. Chantel's bones started to liquefy the instant his hot tongue stroked hers. He had only to kiss her, and she grew weak.

His arms tightened around her, and their kiss deepened. Tyler didn't think he would ever get enough of her. When she eagerly sucked his tongue, his stomach muscles knotted, and his blood rushed through his body like wildfire.

He forced himself to withdraw from their embrace. She'd invited him to dinner, not to bed. If he wasn't careful, Chantel would think he was only interested in sex.

As Tyler slowly released her, his hands gently caressed the silk covering her shoulders and arms. "This feels good," he told her, his tone gruff.

Chantel was still trying to recover from his kiss and decide why he was withdrawing. "Me or the silk?" she asked huskily.

Tyler reached a hand to the button-front of her jumpsuit, and his fingers caressed the bare skin at her throat. "I like you best," he told her.

His touch sent a riot of sensation through Chantel. His simple statement made her feel giddy. He never wasted words, but he made a powerful impact with the ones he chose.

"If you don't stop seducing the chef, you're not going to get any dinner," she warned.

Ty grinned and stepped away from her. "Am I allowed to seduce the chef after dinner?"

"With my blessing," Chantel declared.

They shared a smile full of sensual promise. Then she led him to the kitchen, found a vase for her rose, and placed it in the center of the table.

"Something smells good."

"Lasagna, the frozen kind," she explained. "I have a salad and some Italian bread. Would you like anything else?"

"Sounds fine to me. Can I help?"

"You could pour some drinks."

Tyler poured both of them iced tea. Chantel put the food on the table, and they sat down to eat. During their meal, they exchanged news of their work day, discussed the rotten weather, and finalized their plans for traveling to California.

When they were nearly finished, Chantel remembered the story she'd heard from Donna about Geoff's strange behavior. She told Tyler the details and her suspicion that Geoff had broken into her dad's house.

"Do you think revenge is his motive?" Tyler asked.

"It couldn't have anything to do with me or his job at Cameron," Chantel insisted. "He had to have been planning the break-in before he left the company. He was using me to gain access while we were still on good terms."

"I don't like it."

"Neither do I," she retorted.

"Have you told your dad?"

"Not yet."

"I'll tell him first thing tomorrow. He needs to make sure the house is protected if he's going to be gone for a few days."

"Do you think someone will try to break in again?"

"I doubt it. They've already learned that Aaron's lab is secure, but there's no need to take chances."

"I hope Daddy hired a guard like he promised."

"He hired a firm to watch the property around the clock. They have a good reputation, and Aaron devised a new code system that will alert the police if there's another attempt to force entry to his lab."

"Good," said Chantel. She rose from her chair and started clearing the table. Tyler helped rinse dishes and load the dishwasher. When the kitchen was tidy again, she turned a smile to him.

''I forgot to ask if you'd like dessert.''

''You promised seduction for dessert,'' he reminded, pulling her into his arms.

''Am I supposed to seduce you, or are you going to seduce me?'' she asked lightly. Then a shiver raced over her as he began to nibble on her neck. ''Tyler, you have a habit of making my knees go weak!''

''Is that a complaint?'' he murmured thickly as his nibbling reached her ear.

''Never!'' she swore huskily.

He lifted her in his arms while capturing her mouth with his. Their kiss was long and sweet. Chantel's arms slid around his neck, and she trembled in his arms.

''You're hell on my control,'' Tyler whispered as he carried her to the bedroom.

''Good,'' she returned softly, kissing a path from his chin to his forehead.

Tyler laid her on the bed and switched on the bedside lamp. His eyes were dark with desire, his hands slow. ''I want to do a study of textures,'' he told her hoarsely.

He came down beside her on one knee and cupped her head in his hands. His fingers clenched in the softness of her hair. Then they slipped to the creamy-smooth flesh of her throat. Next they slid over the bodice of her jumpsuit. He felt the sensuous slide of silk, the ripe fullness of her breasts, and finally the thrusting hardness of her nipples.

A low moan escaped Chantel, and Tyler emitted

a matching groan of need. He found one nipple with his mouth and suckled it through a barrier of silk. Chantel moaned again and started to shift restlessly on the bed.

She clutched handfuls of his sweater and tugged it off his body. Tyler's mouth briefly left one breast, but settled on the other in the next instant. His teeth tugged on a taut nipple, and she arched her upper body closer to his mouth. Her fingers convulsively searched the curling hair on his chest to find his nipples. She stroked them until a shudder ripped through Tyler.

He left her just long enough to strip off the rest of his clothes. His breath was coming in agonizing spurts. He could hear the blood pounding in his head and feel it pooling in his groin. He forced himself to control the frenzied desire.

Their eyes smoldered as they met and locked. A primitive need quivered between them. It was stronger than anything either of them had ever known.

Tyler's hands shook as he reached for the buttons between her breasts. A shudder racked him as Chantel's hand slid down his chest, to his stomach, and lower.

"I want to study textures, too," she explained with uneven breaths.

Tyler growled low in his throat. Somehow he managed to remove her clothes. His jaws clenched, and his body shuddered as he fought for control. He was determined to share unhurried lovemaking with her.

That fierce determination nearly drove both of

them insane before their bodies were finally joined and their passion spent.

Chantel knew that Tyler was the most incredible man she'd ever met. He was tender and passionate and unselfish. She knew he cared deeply for her, and she knew she had fallen hopelessly in love with him, but the words were left unsaid.

He wouldn't spend the night. She missed him the instant he was gone, and her sleep was troubled.

ELEVEN

Tyler was waiting in Aaron's office the next morning. He hadn't slept much after leaving Chantel, and he was just as restless and irritable as he had been the previous morning. He wanted more than a love affair with Chantel, much more than an occasional night in her arms, but until things were cleared up he didn't have the right to ask for more.

Aaron entered his office and moved behind his desk. He didn't seem surprised to see Tyler waiting for him.

"What's up?" he asked the younger man.

Aaron sat down, and Tyler rose to his feet. He began to pace as he repeated what Chantel had told him about Geoff Duncan. Aaron's expression grew more grim with every detail.

"So Duncan's behind the attempted robbery."

"That's what Chantel believes."

"He certainly had access to the house," said

166

Aaron. "And to think that he was planning to steal from me while I was making him welcome in my home and was encouraging his relationship with Chantel."

Tyler's expression was tight. Duncan's treatment of Chantel was enough to hang him. "What are you going to do?"

"I'll launch an investigative search into his background. There has to be something important about his past that I missed in an initial study of his qualifications.

"He must have a buyer for the data or he wouldn't have gone to so much trouble to try to steal it. He doesn't have the technical ability to use the research material himself, but he could auction it to the highest bidder."

"Maybe you'll come up with some answers," said Tyler. "I told Chantel I'd warn you to have the house watched while you're gone."

"That's taken care of," Aaron assured him. He was surprised by Ty's uncharacteristic restlessness. "Was there something else?"

"I wanted to tell you that Chantel is going to California with me for the holiday weekend."

Aaron's eyes widened in amazement. "She's going to California with you?" he repeated. "Why?"

"To have Thanksgiving with my family."

Aaron was confused. "What's the purpose?"

"She's going for the holiday because I asked her to. I want her to meet my family."

Aaron had wanted Chantel to make Ty feel at home in Chicago, so why was she encouraging him to go home? He'd wanted the two of them to get better acquainted, but he hadn't anticipated anything more serious.

"Why do you want her to meet your family?"

Tyler dragged a hand through his hair, then stopped pacing and faced Aaron. He looked him directly in the eyes. "Because I'm passionately, desperately in love with her."

The stunned expression on Aaron's face was no less than Tyler had expected. The older man tried to articulate a response, but couldn't seem to find the right words. For a long minute they simply stared at one another.

"You're in love with her?" Aaron finally managed to get the words past his dry throat. "You're in love with her and you want her to go away with you for the weekend. Who'll be acting as chaperon?"

The typically old-fashioned question brought a slight smile to Tyler's lips. Chantel was right about Aaron's view of relationships. She was an independent, intelligent adult, yet her father thought she needed a chaperon. It was time for Aaron to have a realistic view of their relationship.

Tyler chose his words carefully. "We're past needing chaperons, Aaron."

Aaron rose from his chair and glared at Tyler. "What do you mean?"

"I mean I want to make her my wife."

Aaron's eyes widened in shock. His voice was rough when next he spoke. "She's agreed to marry you?"

"I haven't asked her."

"What exactly are your intentions?" Aaron demanded, every inch the outraged parent.

"I can't ask her to marry me with so much deceit between us," Tyler explained, reminding Aaron of the strange circumstances that had thrown Chantel and him together in the first place. "You swore me to secrecy about her adoption and about your being my natural father. I can't ask her to marry me until you release me from those promises."

Aaron slumped back into his chair. The past was catching up with him. He ran a hand over his face and then looked up at his son. Tyler was right. He was a good, honorable man, and he deserved happiness. He and Chantel would be good for each other, but they couldn't have a future until the past was reconciled.

"You love her?"

"Heart and soul."

The succinct response left no room for doubt. The two men continued to stare at each other until Aaron expelled a heavy sigh.

"Would you like me to explain everything to Chantel?" Ty offered.

"No, no. It should come from me," Aaron replied.

Tyler agreed. "Will you get a chance before you leave on your hunting trip?"

Aaron was shaking his head. He wanted a little more time. "I'm leaving at five in the morning to beat the holiday traffic. I can use a few days to find the right words. When will you be back from California?"

"Late Sunday afternoon."

"Why don't you plan to bring her out to the house when you get back. We'll talk then."

Tyler nodded in agreement. He didn't want to put the discussion off so long, but he knew Aaron needed time to come to terms with the situation. He wished he could ease the other man's mind by telling him that Chantel already knew about the adoption. But he'd promised.

"I'll be in my office if you want me."

Aaron watched his son leave with a multitude of conflicting emotions. He'd wanted Ty and Chantel to get to know each other better. He'd even hoped they'd come to love each other, but he hadn't imagined they would fall in love.

They were such opposites. Chantel had sworn off men with an interest in electronics, hadn't she? Ty was such a loner. Chantel was a social butterfly.

Was this all his fault for bribing Chantel in the first place? He'd literally thrown them together. He'd been so desperate to make Tyler proud of his true heritage. Had he made another monumental mistake? Could his children's budding love survive the truth?

The flight to California was uneventful. The sunshine that greeted Tyler and Chantel was warm and welcomed. Tyler rented a car at the Los Angeles airport and drove northward along the coast for almost two hours.

He'd explained to Chantel that his family home was a shorefront cottage built by his dad, Timothy Brogan, who'd been a carpenter by trade.

In reality, the house was a huge, two-storied structure designed to blend with the natural elements of the coastline. Chantel caught her breath at the first sight of the Brogan family home.

"Tyler, it's beautiful!" she exclaimed as he helped her from the car. "How could you leave it for Chicago?"

"I left home a long time before I moved to Chicago," he told her. "The beach is nice, but the house isn't practical for me. I had an apartment closer to work."

She could see his point, but it seemed a shame.

Chantel had worn a royal blue, lightweight wool suit for the flight, and she'd shed her jacket as soon as they landed in the sunshine. Now she worried that her silk blouse was a wrinkled mess. She was suddenly shy about meeting Tyler's family.

"I must look a sight," she told him while trying to smooth some order to her unruly curls. The wind off the water wasn't helping.

Tyler stopped beneath the patio roof. He turned her in his arms and pretended to give her a serious perusal. She was just as lovely as ever. He felt a twinge of panic about introducing her to his brothers.

They'd always been lady-killers. Few women could resist their good looks and easy charm. Ty considered turning around and heading back to Chicago, but he knew it was stupid to be so possessive.

"Well?" Chantel insisted after he'd stared at her for a few minutes. The myriad of emotions in his eyes had made her feel breathless for some reason. She tried to regain her equilibrium. "Am I a mess?"

Tyler drew her into his arms. His eyes were warm, but the conflicting emotions had been suppressed. "It's been a long time since you gave me a kiss," he insisted.

It seemed like an eternity to Chantel. Despite their

lovemaking early in the week, she'd seen too little of him.

"It's been a long time since you asked," she taunted, rising on tiptoe to wrap her arms around his neck and lock her lips with his.

Moans of pleasure mingled in their mouths. Their bodies naturally gravitated closer, her soft curves fitting snugly against his hard angles.

"I've never made love on a beach before," Chantel whispered against his lips.

Her words incited instant arousal in Tyler. He groaned as his body throbbed with excitement. Then he tried to put some distance between them.

Chantel did the opposite. She arched her hips against the rigid evidence of his arousal and simultaneously coaxed his tongue into her mouth. Their kiss was long and sweet.

Tyler finally managed to lift his mouth from hers. "God, Chantel! You make me crazy!"

"Good crazy or bad crazy?" she wanted to know.

"Good," Tyler breathed on a sigh. "So damned good."

"You have the same effect on me," she admitted softly, her eyes sparkling with emotion.

Tyler closed his eyes to block out the sight of her adoring expression. It hurt to see the love and not be secure in it. He didn't have the right to tell her how he felt. Her feelings could change once she'd been exposed to his brothers or learned the truth about his parentage.

The patio door opened, and they eased out of each other's arms. A petite brunette appeared in the doorway with hands propped on her slim hips. Eyes very much like Tyler's teased them.

"I heard the car stop a half hour ago. I wondered what was keeping you."

Tyler slipped an arm about Chantel's waist. "This is the diplomat of the Brogan family: my sister, Marie."

"By diplomat he means I always say what I think, and I think he's been trying to seduce our guest."

"My guest," Tyler reminded. "If you're going to harass Chantel, I'll take her to a nice hotel."

A blush was heating Chantel's cheeks, but she laughed in delight. "Your brother pretends to be such a tyrant. Don't let him browbeat you. I already love it here."

The blush, laughter, and sassy mouth won points with her hostess like nothing else could have done. "The lady obviously has good taste," injected Marie as she held the door open for them.

"She's with me, isn't she?" Tyler taunted arrogantly.

Marie tried to smack him, but he let go of Chantel and wrapped his sister in a bear hug, lifted her off her feet, then planted a loud, smacking kiss on her cheek.

Marie giggled helplessly. "Tyler, let go of me, you're crushing my ribs!" she exclaimed with a gasp.

He eased her feet to the floor and gave her one more kiss on the forehead before releasing her. Marie fought to catch her breath, then berated him.

"You need some lessons in proper decorum," his sister insisted. "And you shouldn't stay away so long!"

Tyler gave her the slashing grin that Chantel loved so much. Seeing him with his sister was a revelation. He insisted he was a loner, but it was obvious that Marie adored her big brother.

"Where are Shawn and Peter?"

"They're playing basketball at the gym, but they'll be home for supper. Are you two hungry?"

"Starved," said Tyler. "But we'll probably survive until we get the luggage inside and get cleaned up. Want to show Chantel her room while I get the bags?"

"Sure," said Marie.

Tyler went back outside, and Marie showed Chantel around the house. It was big, airy, and constructed with walls of windows that let the sunshine pour through the downstairs rooms. The decor was a combination of shiny hardwood and warm earthtones. Chantel thought it was beautiful.

Tyler was delivering her suitcases by the time she finally made it to the second floor bedroom where she'd be sleeping. Marie excused herself, and Tyler ordered Chantel to get into something comfortable and relax.

"I think I'll take a quick shower."

He almost asked if he could join her, but managed to keep the thought to himself. "I'm going to do the same. My room's the last one down the hall on the left. You should have everything you need."

"Marie said dinner will be informal and ready in half an hour," added Chantel. "Shouldn't we help with something?"

"Don't worry about anything. You're supposed to

be on vacation. Besides, Marie loves to cook and she loves to have company.''

"As long as you're sure."

"I'm sure," Ty insisted. "Now how about a kiss to tide me over until I see you again?"

Chantel stepped a little closer to him and dropped a kiss on his lips, then quickly shifted out of reach. "Thank you for bringing my cases. I'll see you in a little while," she told him, her eyes gleaming with devilment.

"Your father's right about you being an incorrigible brat, you know."

Chantel laughed softly and showed him the door. Then she collected clean clothes and headed for the bathroom.

Half an hour later, she finished blow-drying her hair and touched perfume to her wrist and neck. She'd chosen to wear green linen slacks with a short-sleeved knit top in a green floral print.

Tyler had warned her that the evenings could get cool, but Chantel didn't mind a cool sixty degrees compared to Chicago's cool twenty.

She left her room and headed down the hall to the room Tyler had said was his. At her knock, she heard a grunted response. She'd recognize that grunt anywhere, and she assumed it was an invitation to enter.

"Are you decent?" she inquired sweetly while sticking her head in the door.

Tyler was in the process of pulling a yellow knit shirt over his head. Chantel caught only a glimpse of his taut, tantalizing, bare stomach before it was covered. He was wearing jeans, not so old and faded as his painting jeans, but just as form-fitting and sexy.

She stepped inside the door, closed it, and leaned against it while she made an issue of studying him. His hair was slightly damp and mussed from his shower. She had an urge to smooth it, but Tyler reached for a comb before she had a chance to mention the fact.

"I'm almost ready," he told her. "But if you keep looking at me like that, we might not make it to dinner."

His low-throated warning bounced off Chantel like water off a duck. "I like looking at you."

"Do you?" he asked, moving closer. He never got tired of looking at her.

Chantel had both hands behind her back, but her eyes never strayed from him. "Have I told you that I think you're absolutely gorgeous?"

Tyler stopped within arms reach of her, but didn't touch her. His eyes remained locked with hers. "Wait until you meet Shawn and Peter. They're the good-looking ones in the family."

Chantel was shaking her head in disagreement, but her eyes never left his. "They might be drop-dead handsome, but they couldn't be as gorgeous as you."

"Sounds like splitting hairs," he argued.

"Some men are beautiful," Chantel explained, "but then others are gorgeous, with the kind of age-old appeal that women can't seem to resist. That's how you are."

"Irresistible, huh?" Tyler's skepticism was obvious. "What exactly do you find gorgeous or irresistible about me?"

Chantel knew instinctively that he wasn't just fishing for compliments. He wanted to know why she was so attracted to him.

She shifted the few inches until she felt the heat of his body close to hers, but she only touched him with her eyes and hands. "Your hair is so soft and thick, with those sexy little waves that refuse to be restrained." The fingers of both hands stroked his hair, then moved to his cheeks to cradle his face.

"Your eyes are dark, compelling, and usually guarded to refuse anyone a glimpse of the man you are. Your jaw is firm, your chin strong, and your face reflects a strength of character that's more appealing than sheer beauty. You also have a smile that takes my breath away!"

It amazed Ty that she could make him tremble with nothing but words. She reached into his soul and touched him where no other woman had ever explored. How had he lived all these years without her?

Chantel had planned on coaxing a smile from him, but the hands that settled on her waist had a faint tremor in them. Tyler's eyes were turbulent with emotion.

"What happens if you get tired of the same hair, eyes, and face?" he asked. "What happens when the newness wears off? Will you get tired of the smile? Of the guarded emotions?"

He was asking her how much she cared. Chantel didn't know exactly what kind of commitment he wanted from her. They'd never openly declared their love, or discussed the future, so she wasn't ready to bare her heart just yet.

"I think it's going to be a long, long time before I have to face those questions, if ever," she whispered on a soft breath. "In the immediate future, I'm planning to feast on the rest of your gorgeous body!"

Her teasing was intended to break the tension between them, but the ploy failed miserably.

Tyler wrapped her in his arms and kissed her until they were both breathless. His hold on her was crushing, but she didn't utter an objection, she just clutched him in her arms with equal strength. They never seemed to be able to satisfy their consuming need for each other.

Marie's voice calling them to dinner finally penetrated the cocoon of intimacy they'd created. Tyler eased his hold on Chantel, gave her one last, lingering kiss, and then stepped away from her. He dragged in a deep breath to calm himself, then gave her a smile.

"We're being paged."

Chantel was still too breathless to respond, but she returned his smile and turned toward the door. Ty opened it and ushered her out of his room and to the staircase.

"I like your room," she finally remarked, trying to keep it light so that they could recover their poise before facing his family. "I noticed you have three walls of bookshelves."

"Dad and I made a hobby of shelf-building." Tyler was still trying to regain control of his senses.

As they reached the bottom of the stairs and headed toward the kitchen, they encountered Marie, who was coming to call them again.

"I thought maybe you'd gotten lost," she suggested with a knowing glance from Ty to Chantel, then back to Ty.

"We heard you bellow the first time."

"Beast, you're lucky I feed you at all."

"What are you feeding us?" Ty wanted to know. He kept up the lighthearted banter with Marie, giving Chantel more time to recover her composure.

It would have been easier for her if he hadn't grabbed her hand at the foot of the stairs and entwined his fingers with hers. His touch kept her adrenalin high.

At the kitchen doorway, Chantel caught her first sight of Ty's brothers, Shawn and Peter. The two men rose from their seats as she entered the room. At the same time, she lost the comfort of Ty's hand.

"Chantel, meet Shawn and Peter, my baby brothers," said Ty. His remark produced combined groans from the men.

Chantel actually blinked at the sight of them. Ty's brothers were two of the most beautiful men she'd ever seen outside of a theater, yet they didn't look the least bit effeminate. They looked healthy and athletically fit.

Their faces could have been sculpted from the image of Michelangelo's David. They were deeply tanned with dark features like Tyler's, but where he had hard angles, they had smooth edges. She doubted that they had any physical flaws.

"Don't pay any attention to Ty," said one brother with an outstretched hand. "I'm technically younger than him, but only by ten months."

Chantel shook his hand. "Then you must be Shawn," she surmised. She knew Shawn was closest in age to Tyler. "I know you and Peter aren't twins, but I'll bet you've played a few tricks on people over the years."

The only noticeable difference between the brothers was that Shawn's hair grew in tight curls, whereas Peter's was wavy like Tyler's.

"Put a hat on, and we can fool the best of them," declared Peter, reaching out to shake Chantel's hand next.

"I believe it."

"Actually," said Marie with a sister's disrespect for egos. "Shawn's fatter than Peter, and Peter has a louder mouth. I don't have any trouble telling them apart, with or without hats."

Chantel grinned at the good-natured arguing that followed Marie's statement. Tyler held a chair for her, and they all took their places at the table.

Marie had made a taco pie, with tossed salad, tortilla chips, and guacamole dip. It was delicious, but her brothers teased her unmercifully about her cooking.

Conversation throughout dinner was lively. Even though the insults were continuous, Chantel realized the family ties that bound the siblings were strong. They shared a bonding she'd never known as an only child. She couldn't help being a little envious.

Chantel listened with fascination as everyone caught Tyler up to date about their lives, loves, and work. Shawn and Peter were running the family construction business with apparent success.

Marie was an artist who had turned the guest bedroom into a studio. Her paintings were beginning to sell but didn't bring in a lot of money. She was content to cook and keep house for her brothers in exchange for an allowance that supported her painting.

Chantel enjoyed every bite of her meal and every minute of the conversation. She listened, commented occasionally, and laughed a lot. By the end of dinner she felt perfectly comfortable with Tyler's family.

She was aware of Tyler watching her closely throughout the meal. She wondered what he was thinking, but she didn't ask. He said very little except to prompt one of his siblings for more information. It didn't take a genius to realize how much he was loved and respected. With both their parents dead, his brothers and sister seemed to consider him the head of the family.

After their meal, Shawn and Peter invited Tyler, Chantel, and Marie to join them for a beach party, complete with volleyball, a bonfire, and roasting marshmallows. The party was being held at a neighbors about a mile down the beach.

Chantel thought it sounded like fun, but Ty insisted he had some computer files he wanted to study while he was home. She was astounded when he suggested she go without him and wondered why he suddenly wanted to be rid of her. To mask the hurt and confusion of his unexpected rejection, she pretended an interest in the beach party.

_____ TWELVE _____

Marie and Chantel ordered the men from the kitchen while they cleaned the table. Shawn and Peter headed down the beach to help with party preparations. Tyler excused himself and went upstairs to his room.

A short while later, the two women left the house and headed down the short, grassy incline to the beach. From the edge of the water, they could look down the shoreline and see a bonfire. Party music and laughter drifted across the distance.

"I'm sorry, but I've changed my mind. I think I'd rather stay close to the house tonight," Chantel told her hostess. "I hope you don't mind, but I'm a little too tired for a party and meeting a lot of people."

"And you only agreed to come to aggravate Tyler," Marie surmised.

"Exactly," Chantel confessed, then shared a knowing laugh with Marie. "Your big brother is a constant challenge to my patience and sanity."

"He's never been an easy person to get close to," Marie admitted. "Right now you're being subjected to the loyalty test."

"Loyalty test?" Chantel repeated in exasperation. "You mean he deliberately refused to go to the party so that I would have to choose between staying or going?"

"Not exactly," Marie explained. "My brothers have this disgusting little game they play. Whenever one of them gets serious about a woman, they bring her home to meet the other brothers, just in case she might be attracted to one or both. Tyler's giving you a chance to spend time with Shawn and Peter."

"That bum!" snapped Chantel. "I'm absolutely crazy about the man, and he's playing sophomoric games with me!"

Marie laughed softly. "In all fairness, I don't think it's really a game for my brothers. They take it very seriously. Tyler was getting serious about a woman named Susan a few years ago. When she met Shawn, she got serious about him. A few months later, she was serious about Peter."

"Sounds like she was willing to get serious about anybody who gave her the chance," Chantel remarked, bothered by the thought of Tyler with another woman.

"She was emotionally shallow and a real cold fish as far as I was concerned," said Marie. "But she was beautiful, pampered, and appealing to the men."

Chantel grunted. She didn't like it one bit. She didn't like the idea of him caring about that type of woman, she didn't like his lack of faith in her, and she definitely didn't like being tested.

Marie was creating designs in the sand with the toe of her shoe. "I don't want to cause trouble between you and Tyler," she explained hesitantly. "I just didn't want you to be hurt by his attitude."

Chantel watched the sun set over the water and debated about how to handle the situation. She liked Marie and didn't want her to feel guilty for being kind.

"I'll be honest, Marie, and tell you something I haven't even told Tyler. I am madly in love with the man. At this point, I don't think there's anything he could do to change the way I feel about him, but he's going to pay for putting me through his little test."

Marie lifted her head and her eyes met Chantel's. It was growing dark, but they could see each other's grin.

"Have you formulated a plan?" asked Marie.

"You might warn Shawn and Peter that they'll be getting a great deal of my attention tomorrow. Is there any chance there's going to be another party tomorrow night?"

Marie nodded. "It's very likely. I'll threaten my brothers and swear them to secrecy, or they'll tell Tyler what's happening. I hope you'll be careful and not cause any serious problems."

"I'm not going to be too obvious," Chantel promised. "I'm just going to treat them all exactly the same. No special treatment for Tyler, no special smiles or kisses. He's just one of the guys," she added. "We'll see how well he likes that idea."

Marie laughed happily. It was time her brothers learned that women weren't created to be pawns in men's games. She had faith in Chantel's ability to accomplish her objective without causing a family fight.

"You're sure you don't want to join the party for a little while?" Marie asked as she turned to go.

"No thanks," Chantel replied. "I'm beginning to feel the jet lag. I'm going to sit here and enjoy the scenery for a while, then I'm going to bed."

Marie nodded and began to walk down the beach. "See you in the morning," she called softly.

"Have a good night," Chantel responded. Then she eased herself onto the warm sand, wrapped her arms around her knees, and rested her chin on her legs.

She really was tired, tired of body and heart. Tyler's lack of faith in her hurt. She loved him. There was no doubt in her mind about that.

She wasn't going to give up on their relationship without a fight, but she wasn't about to let Tyler play the manipulator. She'd put up with that from her father for too many years. She wouldn't tolerate being manipulated.

Chantel awoke the next morning to the enticing aroma of roasting turkey. The sun pouring through her window was bright, and a glance at her watch told her that it was past ten o'clock. She hadn't intended to sleep so late.

She'd almost forgotten about Thanksgiving and felt guilty for leaving all the cooking and preparations to Marie. She quickly made her bed, took a shower, and dried her hair.

She debated about what to wear. Nobody had mentioned how formally the family dressed for Thanksgiving, but she decided to wear a dress. The only one she'd brought with her was simply styled and suitable for most occasions.

It was a light shade of blue that enhanced the blue of her eyes. The lacy collar was wide and dipped to a v-neck. The shoulders were padded, the sleeves elbow-length. The soft fabric clung to the curves of her breasts, waist, and hips, then fell in gentle folds to her knees.

Chantel matched the dark blue of the dress's belt with dark blue pumps. She didn't plan to wear heels all day, but she figured she could at least start the day with style.

There were no men to be seen as she made her way to the kitchen. She found Marie. Her shoulder-length hair was pulled back in a chignon, and she was busy peeling potatoes. She was also wearing a dress but had it completely enveloped in an apron.

Marie explained that their Thanksgiving dinner was traditionally served at one in the afternoon. Chantel insisted on helping, so an apron was found for her.

Later, all three men miraculously appeared when it was nearly time for dinner to be served. They wore dress pants and knit shirts for the occasion, and were put to work setting the table, pouring drinks, and carrying dishes to the dining room.

Their meal was a huge success. The food was delicious; the conversation was cheerful and lively. Everyone stuffed themselves and then groaned about eating too much. When they finished, Marie informed her brothers that she and Chantel had cooked, so they were responsible for cleaning.

There were more groans, but the men began to clear the table. Chantel and Marie moved into the living room and found easy chairs, then relaxed.

The rest of the day passed quietly with everyone watching parades and football on television. Chantel enjoyed herself, but deliberately annoyed Tyler by refusing to acknowledge the special relationship they shared.

She behaved as though everyone was a new and friendly acquaintance. She teased and shared jokes, yet maintained a measure of reserve, especially where Tyler was concerned.

By evening, she knew he was angry and restless. His eyes speared her with heated little darts of displeasure. When Shawn, Peter, and Marie announced they were going to a party, Chantel suggested that she and Tyler go, too.

"Not tonight," he responded smoothly, rising from his chair to switch off the television.

"Not in the mood?" Chantel taunted. She kept her tone light, but for the first time all day, she let him see a glimpse of the anger she was harboring. "More files to study?"

Tyler's eyes flared with temper. At the sound of the challenge in Chantel's tone, his siblings quietly excused themselves and left the room. The living room was quiet until the outside doors slammed, leaving Tyler and Chantel alone in the house.

"We need to talk." His tone was grim as he faced her.

Hands on hips, eyes flashing, Chantel finally gave vent to her simmering temper.

"About what?" she replied tartly. "About your dragging me a couple thousand miles to test my loyalty? About throwing me into the midst of strangers and then literally abandoning me?"

"Test your loyalty?" Ty questioned with dawning comprehension. "What the hell did Marie tell you?" His sister had doubtlessly incited Chantel's wrath, thus her uncharacteristic behavior.

Chantel ignored the interruption. "About your disgusting, manipulative behavior? About driving me crazy with your hot then cold attitude?" she snapped, truly furious with him for wasting their precious time together with his stupid masculine games.

"I brought you here because I wanted you with me," he stated calmly. The evidence of her outrage had swiftly doused his.

"Well, you have a stinking way of showing it," she snapped. "The first thing you did was throw me at your brothers, as if I were some kind of hot potato you wanted to test for doneness. It's the most ignorant and juvenile act I've ever been a victim of."

Tyler didn't deny her charges. He knew she had every right to be furious. He'd acted like a bastard. During another long, sleepless night without her, he'd realized that the old insecurities didn't matter where she was concerned.

Chantel's righteous indignation was a balm to his emotions after a day of suffering her indifference. The angrier she got, the more confident he felt. He decided to let her vent all her anger before attempting to explain.

She interpreted his calm as insensitivity, and that infuriated her more. "I don't know why you bothered to bring me to California, Tyler Brogan, but I tell you this . . . as much as I like your family, I'm not staying anywhere near you for any longer than I have to! I'm calling the airport and catching the next flight home!"

Chantel swung away from him and strode toward the telephone. She was punching in an information code when she felt Tyler step close behind her.

His hand covered hers on the receiver. "Please don't," he coaxed.

His touch sent a quiver of awareness up her arm. His deep, husky voice whispered along her nerve endings. The heat of his body permeated hers, and the melting process began. Chantel steeled herself against the attraction. She wasn't going to let him win so easily.

"There's no reason for me to stay," she insisted, then asked an operator for the airport number.

After Chantel replaced the receiver, but before she could dial the airport, Tyler eased her hand off the phone and carried it to her waist. He wrapped his other arm around her and drew her back against his chest, then buried his face beneath the hair at her neck.

"Would it help if I swear I'm sorry?" he asked while nuzzling her neck with warm lips.

His touch sent chills over her body. Chantel was weakening, but she knew if she didn't hold on to her anger she'd break down in tears.

"Sorry for what?" she insisted. "Sorry for being a total jerk?"

Tyler recognized the hurt replacing the anger in her tone. He wanted to kiss her and make it better, but he knew she needed an explanation for his strange behavior.

"What if I told you that I care so much it scares the hell out of me?"

Chantel closed her eyes in defeat. A few of his well-chosen words always turned her willpower to mush. She loved him with an intensity that was beyond her experience. If he felt the same, she could understand his wariness to believe it was real and reciprocated.

Tyler's lips continued their foray up her neck to her throat. Chantel tipped her head back against his shoulder to allow him free access. Despite his apparent calm, she could feel the tremor of his body as he drew her closer.

She desperately wanted to declare her love, to assure him that he didn't have to worry about her loyalty. But even though he'd said he cared, he hadn't mentioned love, so neither did she. Maybe he wasn't comfortable with the term. Maybe he couldn't differentiate between the physical and emotional loving.

"Are you going to forgive me and let me make it up to you?" Tyler asked as he nibbled the corner of her lips.

"Probably."

Tyler wanted to destroy all her resistance. "What will it take to change a probable into an absolute?"

Chantel turned in his arms and flattened her hands on his chest. She tilted her head slightly, and their eyes locked. Hers were still guarded. His smoldered with emotion—hot, primitive, needy emotion.

Liquid heat poured through her, and Chantel lost all desire to argue. She wanted him to make love to her, and he obviously wanted the same thing.

"Tell me what you want, Chantel," he pleaded, his tone thick with feeling. "Anything."

One gruff word from him prompted another expressive one from her, "Kiss."

The word was barely out of her mouth before his lips slammed against hers. There was no gentleness, no tentative tasting, just honest, ravenous hunger. His tongue thrust through her teeth and boldly challenged her tongue to a duel.

Mouths mated hungrily. Arms tightened reflexively. Hands stroked convulsively. Tyler drew her between his legs and crushed her against the cradle of his thighs. They couldn't get close enough, regardless of how hard they strained.

He moaned, she sobbed, and they both struggled for breath. "Let me take you to bed," rasped Tyler. "Let me love you. Please."

"Yes, yes, yes," Chantel whispered against his lips.

They climbed the stairs slowly because neither of them had enough strength in their legs to make it alone. The long, slow climb gave them an opportunity to kiss and caress, but the caresses became more frantic when they reached Tyler's room and struggled out of their clothes.

They were on fire for one another, their passion raged out of control, and neither of them made an effort to halt the headlong rush toward sensual pleasure.

Tyler joined their bodies in the most intimate fashion and cried out with the ecstasy of sheathing himself in her softness. Chantel accepted him with a gasp; the pleasure was so intense that she shuddered. She matched his rhythm with every ounce of strength she possessed, then clutched him feverishly as they found satisfaction.

. When they'd regained some measure of control, Tyler gently cradled Chantel in his arms and began to arouse her all over again. While he stroked her smooth, damp skin, he tried to explain why he found it hard to express his deepest feelings.

"I've always been a possessive person," he told her as he licked the shell of her ear.

His mouth roved over the familiar curves of her face. "I've been told by several women that I smothered them with my possessiveness. I didn't want to do that to you."

"You have my permission to smother," Chantel insisted as his mouth created a renewed ache deep inside her.

"I've also been accused of having an insatiable sexual appetite," he warned as his mouth drifted over the slope of her breast to find a nipple.

Chantel resented any woman having that kind of knowledge about her man. She would have complained, but Tyler drew her nipple deep into his mouth and sucked until she forgot her objections.

"Tyler!" she exclaimed huskily, clenching her fingers in his hair as he shifted his attention to the other nipple.

His blood was beginning to pound heavily through his veins again. Chantel was so responsive. He could feel her growing restless in his arms.

"You don't mind if I'm insatiable?" he ground out roughly, letting her drag his head up for a kiss.

"No! No! No!" she chanted, kissing him feverishly. She was beginning to believe she could be insatiable, too, especially where he was concerned.

"You're sure?" he demanded as they fought for air.

"Positive," she bit out breathlessly.

"Then we can make love all night?"

"Yes! Yes! Yes!"

And they did. They made wild, uninhibited love, then lazy, erotic love, then more wild, uninhibited love. It was almost dawn before they fell asleep in each other's arms.

Chantel knew it was after noon when she woke the next day. The sun was bathing the bed where she and Tyler were sprawled in a tangle of sheets. She'd never felt so sensitive, so sexual, or so special in her life. Tyler had spent the night proving how much he needed her, and she'd fallen more deeply in love than she'd thought possible.

For a long time, she just watched him sleep. He was so gorgeous. She loved every inch of his body from his tousled, wavy hair to the curly hair on his naked toes.

It took great effort to keep from waking him, but she could imagine what his family must be thinking. It might be accurate, but it was still embarrassing. It would only get worse if she and Tyler stayed in bed much longer.

He continued to breathe deeply as she slipped from bed and gathered her clothes. After peeking out the door to ensure the hallway was clear, she dashed to her room and took a quick shower. Dressed in yellow cotton shorts and a matching t-shirt, she headed downstairs to see if anyone else was in the house.

The sound of several voices from the kitchen drew an inaudible moan from Chantel. Just her luck. It was lunch time and Tyler's siblings were all seated at the table.

Chantel commanded herself not to blush as she entered the kitchen. She expected teasing and embarrassing questions, but all she received were quiet greetings.

Shawn and Peter didn't look like they'd been awake much longer than her. Marie was the only one who didn't look hungover.

"Good morning. Can I get you something to eat?"

"Sit still," Chantel told her as she moved to the refrigerator. "I just want something cold to drink."

She poured herself a tall glass of orange juice and intended to go outside to the patio table, but Tyler chose that moment to enter the kitchen.

Their eyes met, and a shiver of awareness danced along Chantel's flesh. He looked like a man who hadn't gotten any sleep and didn't mind. All he was wearing was a pair of ragged cut-off jeans. The rest of him was gloriously, sensuously naked. His hair was still tousled, his eyes slumberous. Chantel had to remind herself to breathe.

The three people at the table seemed to perk up when Ty entered the room. He headed for the coffee-pot, filled a cup, then leaned against the counter while he took the first tentative sip.

Chantel decided not to leave. Instead, she leaned

casually against the refrigerator and faced Tyler. "Good morning," she said to him.

Tyler didn't waste words, but his smile was slow and sensual. His eyes gleamed with mesmerizing warmth—sexy, evocative, masculine warmth that heated the very core of her.

Chantel couldn't drag her eyes from him. His shoulders were so appealingly broad, his chest was covered with dark, curling hairs, and his long legs were so strong. If she'd thought him gorgeous before, it was nothing compared to the way she felt about him since she'd had a chance to explore every inch of his vibrantly male body.

"I take it you won the disagreement over the loyalty test," Marie said to Chantel.

Tyler frowned and flashed an irritated glance at his sister, but when Chantel spoke, she had his total attention.

"I don't think that little game has anything to do with loyalty," she declared boldly, her eyes locking with Tyler's. "I think just the opposite is true."

"Do you?" Tyler challenged.

"I'd bet my Lamborghini on it," she returned smugly.

"Lamborghini?" Shawn and Peter chorused.

"You don't have a Lamborghini," Tyler reminded, watching her over the top of his coffee mug.

Chantel grimaced. "I know. My daddy never would buy me one."

"What do you mean by just the opposite?" asked Marie.

"I don't think the Brogan men are so worried about losing a woman's affections. I think they're more worried about having one get too close to their hearts.''

Tyler's eyes flashed at the challenge in her tone, and he arched a brow but didn't comment.

"I'm inclined to agree with that conclusion," remarked Shawn as he rocked backward on two legs of his chair. "Ever since old Susan tried to slip the noose over Ty's head, I've known that he deliberately sicced her on me."

"Yeah," spouted Peter. The sound of his own voice made him wince, but he continued. "And when the noose got close to Shawn's neck, he tried to slip it over to mine."

"So you have it all figured out, do you?" Tyler drawled dangerously.

Chantel drained the last of her juice and set the glass in the sink. "I've got it all figured out," she boasted. She leaned against the sink and crossed her arms over her chest. Her eyes dared him to deny the charges.

Tyler moved slowly to the sink and rinsed out his mug. "I'm taking a shower," was his only response.

When he turned and started to leave the room, Chantel got in one last quip. "Need any help?" she whispered just loud enough for him to hear.

Tyler stopped, turned, and had her in his arms before she could react. "As a matter of fact, I do," he taunted.

"It was a joke, Tyler," Chantel squealed as he hauled her into his arms and carried her from the kitchen. "A joke, Tyler, really. I was teasing."

When he ignored her and headed for the stairs, she clung to him and changed tactics. "I really don't need a shower, Tyler,'' she insisted in a pleading tone. ''I already had one. I'm all dressed. I don't want to get my hair wet again.''

Tyler stopped at the top of the stairs and looked directly into her eyes. ''I woke up lonely,'' he complained.

Chantel grinned. ''I was tempted to wake you,'' she told him. ''But I thought you might want to sleep.''

''I want you.''

''Now?'' she asked softly.

''Always.''

''Promise?''

''Promise.''

THIRTEEN

Their flight left Los Angeles in the morning, but it was late afternoon before they had their luggage loaded in Tyler's car at Midway Airport in Chicago.

"Your dad wanted me to bring you out to his house when we got home today. Is that a problem?" Tyler asked Chantel when they'd cleared the worst of the airport traffic.

"No, I don't mind."

"Do you want to stop by your apartment first?"

Chantel shook her head. "There's no need to go there first. I can unpack later."

"Will you be warm enough?"

Tyler had on a leather jacket, but Chantel was only wearing a cotton windbreaker. They'd come home to cold, damp weather.

"I'll be fine once the car's warm, and I have coats at Daddy's if I need one later."

"You want my jacket now?"

It was the third time he'd asked her the same question. Chantel gave him a smile. "No, thank you."

Tyler took his eyes from the road long enough to flash her an answering smile. "I don't want you to suffer from weather shock."

"It's a shock all right," Chantel grumbled. "I don't know how you can stand to leave California."

"Chicago has its attractions," he told her.

"Name one."

"You."

Chantel laughed in delight. She'd never been so happy in her whole life. She and Tyler had spent the last two days playing on the beach and falling deeper in love. He still hadn't actually said the word, but she didn't doubt the strength of his feelings.

"Don't forget Cameron Industries," she insisted playfully.

It amazed Tyler that he hadn't given the business a thought for days. When he was with Chantel, nothing else seemed important. She was addictive, and he was already having withdrawal symptoms. He didn't want to consider how she might react to Aaron's news.

Tyler broke out in a sweat when he thought about losing her completely. The closer they got to Aaron's, the greater his panic. He didn't want anything to hurt her. She was the sweetest, most giving person he'd ever met.

He wanted to protect her from the pain and confusion of learning that he was Aaron's biological son. He wanted to use his love as a protective shield, but he was afraid she might resent him even more. He could only pray that she had enough faith in him to know he wouldn't do anything to deliberately hurt her.

When they turned into Aaron's driveway, Chantel unsnapped her seatbelt and slid closer to Tyler. He'd been so quiet that it worried her. She rested a hand on his arm and felt the tension in him.

"What's wrong?" she asked, her eyes searching his.

Tyler parked the car, turned off the ignition, and turned to her. He pulled her into his arms and hugged her fiercely, rubbing his face in the softness of her hair.

Chantel slipped her arms inside his jacket and hugged him tightly. Her face was pressed against his neck, and she kissed it softly.

"Tyler, what's wrong?" she asked again when he remained silent, but he didn't ease his death grip on her.

Ty forced himself to relax and gradually released her. Their eyes locked, and he cupped her face in his hand.

"I love you."

Chantel's heart skipped a beat, then began to pound. Her blood raced through her body at an alarming rate.

"I know that," she replied huskily. It was what she didn't know that was scaring her.

Tyler slid his hand into her hair. His fingers clutched the silky strands. He didn't want to stop touching her. He couldn't bear the thought of losing her.

"Please, Tyler, tell me what's wrong," Chantel

begged. "Is it Daddy? Has something happened to him? Something you don't want to tell me about?"

Ty shook his head. "I haven't heard anything from Aaron, but the reason he wanted me to bring you out here is because he needs to tell you something. I'm afraid it's going to hurt you."

Chantel had never seen Tyler so shaken. She knew he was hurting for her, but she couldn't imagine what her dad had to say.

"Is the company going under? Is he going to sell it? Is he losing the house, or going bankrupt?"

Tyler shook his head. "It's nothing like that, and I promised not to say anything. I just want you to know how much I love you. Nothing's going to change that. Ever."

"I love you, too," she declared softly. "Nothing's going to change that. Whatever's wrong, we can handle it."

Tyler groaned as he captured her lips with his hungry mouth. He kissed her deeply, lovingly, thoroughly, and then he forced himself to let her go. He was only prolonging the agony. She had to learn the truth or they had no future.

"Aaron didn't see you before we left, so he gave me your key. It's for the new locks," Tyler said, his tone devoid of emotion. "He told me the new code and wrote it down for you. I have it in my wallet. I'll give it to you later."

With that, he climbed from the car and strode around to her side, then opened her door.

His strange behavior had Chantel too worried to concentrate on keys and codes. She briefly wondered why they hadn't encountered the security guard her dad had hired, but the thought was fleeting.

Tyler rang the doorbell to alert Aaron of their arrival. He used the key and recited the entry as he punched the numbers. Chantel didn't even try to memorize them.

She entered the house first and called out to her dad. Tyler reset the alarm and followed her into the living room. The lights were on, but Aaron wasn't anywhere in sight. He didn't respond to her calls.

"He's probably in his lab," she said.

"I'll go check."

"We'll go check," she countered, slipping an arm through his arm.

When they approached the door of the lab, Chantel stopped abruptly and tugged on Tyler's arm. She put her finger to her lips to warn him not to speak. Then she pointed to the door of her dad's lab. It was standing wide open. He never left it open. Something wasn't right.

Ty gently eased her flat against the wall and silently insisted she stay out of sight. He carefully approached the door.

"I know you're out there!" shouted a rough, unfamiliar voice. "You better get in here or the old guy dies."

Chantel gasped softly, then covered her mouth with her hand. Her eyes widened in horror as Tyler stepped through the doorway to the lab.

A tall, thin man with a stocking mask had a tight hold on the back Aaron's shirt. In his other hand was a gun pointed at Aaron's head. Both men faced Tyler as he entered the room.

"Get in here," said the intruder, waving the gun to demonstrate his impatience. "Where's the woman? I heard a woman!"

"She went upstairs to the bathroom," Tyler lied. He looked directly at Aaron. "What's going on?"

"Whoever failed to get my data last time hired this guy to do his dirty work," Aaron explained.

"Shut up!" snarled the armed man. "Get the woman in here! I want everybody where I can see 'em."

Chantel had heard enough. She knew that hiding wouldn't help matters. She didn't know how the intruder was subduing her dad, but she didn't want to do anything that would further aggravate the thief.

"I'm right here," she declared as she stepped in the door. Tyler and Aaron both hissed their disapproval, but she moved into the room.

"Get over by him," the intruder commanded, waving his gun in Ty's direction.

Chantel moved toward Tyler. When she was close enough, he grabbed her arm and gently shoved her behind him.

The armed man released Aaron. He pointed his gun at Tyler and snarled at Aaron. "Now get busy and fill that briefcase or I'll kill them both."

Aaron did as he was told, but now the intruder had to divide his attention between two targets. He was getting increasingly nervous. His whole body was twitching restlessly as he waved the gun back and forth between them.

The lab was eerily silent except for the rustle of papers. Chantel could hear the blood pounding riotously in her head. Tyler was as still as stone. She prayed he wouldn't do anything risky.

They all heard the wail of sirens at the same time.

"What the hell?" rasped the gunman. "You set off a silent alarm?" he charged as he swung the gun toward Aaron.

The next few minutes became a blur for Chantel. She saw her dad's briefcase being hurled toward the gun. In the same instant, Tyler flew across the room. The gun went off, and she screamed in terror. Then Tyler and the gunman were on the floor wrestling for control of the gun.

Chantel instinctively searched the room for some sort of weapon to use against the intruder. Aaron was trying to get close enough to the fighting men to get hold of the gun.

There was grunting and cursing as the men rolled around the floor. Then Tyler was on top of the gun-man, slamming the hand holding the gun to the floor. The gun went off again, but Aaron quickly stamped on the gunman's wrist and forced him to release the weapon. The thud of fists connecting with flesh and bone sent a shudder of revulsion through Chantel.

"I've got the gun, Tyler," Aaron shouted, then turned to Chantel. "Go let the police in."

Tyler managed to bring a fist down on the side of the intruder's head, and he abruptly went limp. Chantel ran for the door. When she brought the po-lice back to the lab, Aaron had the gun pointed at the would-be thief, and Tyler was pulling the man to his feet. He jerked the mask off his head, but the man was a total stranger to all of them.

The police, however, recognized him. "So you're

causing trouble again, Bowser." They swiftly had the man handcuffed and read him his rights.

"You know this guy?" Aaron asked the officer in charge.

"He's a two-bit hood for hire. Have any idea who might have hired him and why?"

Aaron began to explain the situation to the police. Tyler had backed out of the way when help arrived. He was leaning against a wall, and Chantel rushed to his side.

His breathing was still labored, and he was deathly pale. His lip was cut and his jaw bruised. She grabbed his hands and realized they were cut and bleeding, too.

Her action brought a moan from Tyler, and her eyes widened in fear. He was in serious pain. "Tyler!" she cried, searching him with her hands to find the source of his pain.

Then she saw the dark stain on his jacket. She gently shifted the leather aside and gasped in shock. The whole left side of Tyler's torso was soaked in blood.

"Daddy! Tyler's been shot!" she yelled, halting all other discussion. "Get the paramedics!"

Chantel was shoved aside when men rushed to Tyler's assistance. Her eyes sought his, and he gave her a weak smile. "It's high on my arm," he assured her. "Not too bad."

The gunshot might have missed vital organs, but it had obviously hit a major vein. Blood continued to pour from the wound until the medics could halt the flow. As soon as they were sure Tyler was stabilized and not going into shock, they strapped him to a stretcher and loaded him in the ambulance. Chantel rode with him to the hospital. Aaron followed in a police cruiser.

It seemed like the longest ride she'd ever taken. Tyler was conscious and doing his best to comfort her, but Chantel had never been so frightened in her life. She couldn't stop shaking.

As soon as they reached the hospital, Tyler was wheeled into an examining room. He was shifted from the stretcher to an examination table. The paramedics left, and a harried-looking doctor came in to examine his arm.

"Looks like you lost a lot of blood," said the doctor. "Do you know your blood type?"

Tyler shot a strange glance at Chantel and mumbled something to the doctor. He was asked to repeat the information and complied in a more audible tone. She heard him the second time and was surprised to learn that he had the same unusual blood type as her father.

Chantel tried to stay out of everyone's way. Tyler kept giving her strange looks, and she wondered if he was in pain but didn't want to alarm her.

Aaron came rushing into the emergency room, saw Chantel, and headed in her direction. She nodded toward the cubicle where Tyler was being treated.

"Doctor, I'm Aaron Cameron," he told the young intern. He stepped closer to see Tyler's wound as the doctor removed the medic's bandaging. "He was shot by a .38 caliber handgun at close range. If he needs blood, I can donate. My blood is a perfect match. We had tests run a year ago."

Tyler growled something, and Aaron turned horrified eyes to Chantel. At first she didn't understand why her dad looked so upset. Her immediate reaction was fear that Tyler was more seriously hurt than the paramedics had implied.

Then it hit her. It hit hard because she was under an enormous amount of stress. Her dad and Tyler shared the same rare blood type. She stared from one of them to the other. Their blood was a perfect match. They'd had blood tests made. A slow, dawning realization drained every ounce of blood from her face.

"No!" she refused to believe her own suspicions, but the identical expressions of concern on Tyler's and Aaron's faces sent a shock wave over her body.

"Chantel," Aaron started toward her.

She reached out a hand to ward him off. Her other hand was clasped over one ear as if to forbid the words she didn't want to hear. Her wounded eyes shifted from Aaron back to Tyler. Tyler.

His eyes were wild with emotion. He slid off the bed and tried to stand, but he was too unsteady. The doctor quickly steadied him and ordered him to be still.

Chantel's heart was pounding erratically, and she knew she had to be alone until she could make some sense of what she'd just learned.

A police officer approached Aaron and tapped him on the shoulder. Chantel turned and ran from the emergency room. She found a quiet waiting room and sank into a plastic sofa, then curled her legs under her and dropped her head to her knees.

Tyler was her father's son. His biological son. That fact was the missing piece to the puzzle. Now she understood why Tyler had agreed to move to Chicago. She understood why her dad had been so adamant about making Tyler want to stay.

She understood so many other things: the surprising rapport between the two men, Aaron's absolute trust in Tyler, the shared interests, the natural genius for electronics. They had so much in common.

They'd had blood tests made last year. Was that how long they'd known? Was that how long they'd kept the truth from her?

Chantel's head throbbed unmercifully, making it hard to think. Still, she could feel. And she hurt. Why hadn't they trusted her with the truth? What possible reason could they have had to keep her in the dark? What threat could she pose to either of them? She just wanted to love them.

Love. Tyler had told her he loved her. Finally. He'd told her this evening before they went into her dad's house. He'd said her dad was going to tell her something important, but she'd forgotten in all the excitement.

Had they planned to tell her together? Hopefully. Tyler had been really worried about her reaction to the news, and she understood why. They'd been as close as two people could be, yet he hadn't hinted at a secret that might destroy her faith in their future. She loved him desperately. Why couldn't he have trusted her just a little?

There were no easy answers. Chantel knew she wasn't Aaron's biological daughter, so Tyler's parentage had little effect on their relationship. Belatedly, she remembered that her dad didn't know about her knowledge of the adoption. She'd sworn Tyler to secrecy. Had he kept his promise?

He'd made love to her before she'd told him that Aaron wasn't her real father. He must have known the truth about her illegitimacy from the beginning. Aaron must have told him she was adopted. Obviously, they trusted each other. Why didn't they trust her?

It was almost two hours later when Tyler found Chantel. He'd been given a pint of Aaron's blood and felt some of his strength returning. His arm hurt like hell. The doctor had wanted to sedate him, but he wanted Chantel.

She was curled in a fetal position on a short, ugly sofa. Her head was resting on her knees, and a tumble of curls hid her face from him. Tyler grimaced at the sight of his blood staining her clothes. He approached her slowly and eased himself down beside her.

The movement startled Chantel. She'd dozed off to sleep, but now she awakened abruptly. "Tyler," she said drowsily, her eyes going directly to his shoulder. "Should you be out of bed?"

"It's just a surface wound," he explained. "The bullet didn't lodge in my arm, so all they had to do was take a couple of stitches."

The thought of his flesh being torn by a bullet made Chantel nauseous. She closed her eyes until her stomach stopped rolling.

"I broke my promise." Tyler didn't know how else to broach the subject. He couldn't stand to see her hurting.

Chantel reopened her eyes and stared into his. "Which promise?"

"I told your dad that you already knew about the adoption," he began, never taking his eyes from her.

"The only reason he didn't tell you about me was because he didn't want you to think we were brother and sister. He didn't see any reason for you to know the truth about your birth since your biological father was dead. He was afraid you might be devastated by the truth, or that you might think less of your mother."

Chantel made a rasping sound of denial. "How could he think that?"

"He'd kept the secret for so long that he didn't know how to tell you, and he was afraid."

"He said you had blood tests made a year ago," Chantel whispered, tears threatening. "How could you keep something like this from me?"

Tyler closed his eyes and leaned his head wearily against the wall. He began to explain the series of events that had brought him to Chicago. He told her about his mother's deathbed confession, his initial meeting with Aaron, the blood tests, his dissatisfaction with his position in California, and Aaron's desire for him to take control of Cameron Industries.

"I knew a relationship between the two of us could lead to trouble," he admitted quietly, holding Chantel's gaze with unflinching steadiness, "but Aaron wanted us to get to know each other better."

They had done that. "He obviously didn't mean to play matchmaker," surmised Chantel.

"No, he was definitely surprised when I told him

how I felt about you," Tyler said, shifting his eyes to the bare wall opposite the sofa.

Chantel's eyes searched his beloved features. "When did you tell him?" It was important to her.

Tyler's eyes swung back to her. "I told him before we left for California." When her eyes filled with tears he felt his heart bleeding. "I told him I loved you, and that I wanted to marry you, but you had to know the whole truth first. I didn't want to hurt you." A weary sigh escaped. He'd certainly failed to protect her from the pain.

"That's what you were trying to warn me about, wasn't it? Daddy was planning to tell me tonight, wasn't he?"

"Yes."

"Where is he now?"

"He went to the police department to file an official report on the break-in. They're sure that Bowser character will tell who hired him. Aaron's sure it's Duncan."

"What happened to Daddy's security guard?"

"They found him bound and gagged in the field behind the house."

Chantel grunted, and it startled them both. Tyler grinned, and her heart felt lighter than it had all night. Her answering smile was a little shaky. Their eyes met and exchanged intimate messages.

"Have I told you how much I love your smile?" she whispered, reaching out to him for the first time since he'd joined her.

Tyler caught her hand and carried it to his mouth. He kissed each finger. "Have I told you how much I love you?" he asked in a tone hoarse with emotion.

Chantel closed her eyes to delay more tears. "I'm never going to hear it enough," she swore hoarsely.

Tyler wrapped his right arm around her shoulders. Chantel uncurled her legs and slid close enough to rest her head on his good shoulder. Someone had loaned him a clean shirt. It was thin and had already taken on the heat and scent of his body. She snuggled closer.

"Would you consider letting me tell you how much I love you for another fifty or sixty years," he asked while stroking her hair with unsteady fingers.

"Is that a proposal?"

"It is if you accept," he told her softly, his chest tight with fear. "If you don't, then it's just the beginning of an endless campaign to win your trust. I love you more than you'll ever know, and I want you to be my wife."

Chantel pressed a hand against his heart. "I love you, too, and I accept your proposal," she whispered. "Just don't ever scare me again like you did tonight. I couldn't survive without you, and I don't intend to try."

Tyler groaned softly and hugged her tighter. He buried his face in her hair while he fought to control the wave of emotion her words evoked.

"Can you forgive Aaron and me for not telling you the truth as soon as we found out?"

Chantel was quiet for a long time. Then she tilted her head so that she could look him in the eyes. "I know you macho males think it's your responsibility to protect me, but I won't tolerate the two of you making decisions and trying to manipulate me," she declared with a return of spirit.

Tyler tried to hide his grin by gently pulling her head against his chest.

His smile was one of the first things Aaron saw upon entering the room. The fact that Chantel was cuddled against Tyler lent him hope that she'd forgive him, too. He moved closer to the sofa before speaking.

"Chantel?"

Her head shot up, and she looked straight at her father. He seemed to have aged ten years in the past few hours. Her heart went out to him.

"Daddy!" she exclaimed softly. Then she gently untangled herself from Tyler's embrace and leapt off the sofa into her father's arms. He hugged her tightly, and she hugged him with equal strength. Aaron gave Tyler a watery smile of thanks for whatever he'd said on his behalf.

"I want you to know that I have never, ever done anything to deliberately hurt you," he whispered gruffly.

"I know that."

"Can you forgive your old man for being a little too protective?"

"A little?" Chantel repeated, easing her death grip on him.

"You shouldn't have asked that," said Tyler. "She's got a lecture prepared for how she expects to be treated in the future."

"With respect!" Chantel retorted sassily. She searched her pockets for a handkerchief, then accepted one from her dad. "Thank you."

"What did you find out about the burglary?" Tyler wanted to know.

"Duncan was behind it. Bowser implicated him, and he confessed. It seems he's a very distant relative of the Anderson family, and he wanted a hand in running the family business. He was given a low-level job, but he wasn't satisfied to work his way up the ladder."

"He thought stealing your research would elevate his level of importance?" asked Tyler.

"He'd heard rumors of my work and intended to hire someone to build a similar robot. Then he'd try to pass the work off as his own."

"Did he really think that Andersons' board of directors would be stupid enough to believe him once it was known that your data had been stolen?" Chantel asked.

"At first he didn't plan a robbery. He just wanted to get into my lab and photograph the data. That way I wouldn't have any proof of theft."

"But he failed at his first attempt and was too stupid to give up."

"That's about the size of it."

"I can't believe he sent an armed man to your house," said Chantel in disgust.

"He swears he told Bowser not to hurt anyone," Aaron explained. "But he was glad that Tyler took a bullet if anyone had to."

Chantel made a noise that sounded very much like a grunt. Both men lifted a brow, and she realized how much alike they were.

"You're the one who told me to befriend Tyler," she reminded her dad. "It's your fault if his bad habits are rubbing off on me."

Aaron smiled, then grew serious again. "Do you

think you can get used to the idea of him being my son?''

"If you can get used to the idea of him being your son-in-law, as well," Chantel replied, then walked over to Tyler's side.

Aaron looked startled, then shot a glance at Tyler. "So, she's agreed to marry you."

Tyler nodded and reached a hand out to Chantel. "She tagged on a few stipulations, but nothing I can't live with," he teased.

Chantel laughed softly. "Are you going to sit there all night, or can we go home?"

"Actually, I don't think I can get up."

"Oh! Tyler!" Chantel exclaimed on a laugh. "Help me, Daddy. Our poor, brave invalid is stuck to the plastic."

"You'll pay for that," he threatened as Aaron and Chantel carefully helped him to his feet, trying not to jolt his bad arm any more than necessary.

"One of the patrolmen brought Tyler's car to the hospital," Aaron told them. "I'll go bring it up to the emergency entrance."

Aaron left the room, and they were momentarily alone. "I thought he'd never leave," Tyler whispered as he gathered her to him. "I haven't had a kiss for hours."

"I think I can fix what ails you," she murmured as her lips made their way up his chin to his mouth. Their kiss was long, and deep, and sweetly satisfying.

"I'm going to need a lot of TLC for the next few days," he suggested when their mouths finally parted.

"Want me to hire you a nurse?" she teased, her eyes filled with love and danced with mischief.

"I want you." Tyler's reply was short and to the point.

He trapped her moan of delight between their mouths. Then he kissed her until one of the medical staff came to tell them their ride was waiting.

EPILOGUE

Chantel was a Christmas bride. As she walked down the aisle with Aaron, Tyler's heart swelled with pride and a love too deep to put into words. He adored her: her enchanting laughter, her compassionate heart, her lively sense of humor, and her unquestionable loyalty.

Chantel walked toward Tyler without a doubt in her mind regarding their future. She knew the love they shared was the everlasting kind. She knew Tyler would always stand by her side. He was strong and brave, tough and tender, passionate, yet sensitive. Her love for him was endless.

Aaron placed Chantel's hand into Tyler's. Despite his love and respect for his newly found son, it was one of the hardest things he'd ever done in his life. He gave her a kiss and turned from the altar with tears in his eyes.

A slight tremor shook Tyler's hand as he placed

the ring on Chantel's finger. Her fingers were trembling, too. They repeated their vows with a full understanding of what they promised each other. The groom kissed his bride with a possessive tenderness that showed her, and a church full of onlookers, how much she was cherished.

The reception went on for hours. Tyler's family was getting their first experience with winter in Chicago, and they'd accepted an invitation to spend their Christmas vacation with Aaron. Tyler and Chantel would be enjoying a honeymoon on the beach in California.

Mr. and Mrs. Tyler Brogan would spend their wedding night at the bride's apartment in Chicago, but they didn't publicize the fact.

When Chantel was dressed in her traveling clothes, she found Tyler. Hand in hand, they approached Aaron.

"We're going to leave now, Daddy," she whispered, giving him a kiss.

Aaron wrapped her in his arms and hugged her tightly. His eyes sparkled with emotion as they met Tyler's.

"You take good care of my baby," he commanded gruffly. He released Chantel and teased both his children. "Just remember, husbands can be dumped, but daddies are forever."

Tyler grunted. "This husband's forever," he pledged.

"Besides," Chantel reminded as she swiped at happy tears. "You're not losing a daughter, you're gaining a son."

No. 71 ISLAND SECRETS by Darcy Rice
Chad has the power to take away Tucker's hard-earned independence.

No. 72 COMING HOME by Janis Reams Hudson
Clint always loved Lacey. Now Fate has given them another chance.

No. 73 KING'S RANSOM by Sharon Sala
Jesse was always like King's little sister. When did it all change?

No. 74 A MAN WORTH LOVING by Karen Rose Smith
Nate's middle name is 'freedom' . . . that is, until Shara comes along.

No. 75 RAINBOWS & LOVE SONGS by Catherine Sellers
Dan has more than one problem. One of them is named Kacy!

No. 76 ALWAYS ANNIE by Patty Copeland
Annie is down-to-earth and real . . . and Ted's never met anyone like her.

No. 77 FLIGHT OF THE SWAN by Lacey Dancer
Rich had decided to swear off romance for good until Christiana.
